KING OF THE HILL

by

Timothy Johnstone

King of the Hill

The following is a work of fiction. Any references to past events, real people and places, and incidents are from the author's imagination.

ISBN: 978-0-578-28668-6 (Paperback)

Library of Congress Control Number: 2022906443

Front cover design by: Michael Coller

Timajohn11@gmail.com

With gratitude to my wife Vicki, and to Landon and Trent.

Thanks for your love, support and inspiration.

1

Tigers' second baseman TJ Jones was as nervous as a long-tailed cat in a room full of rocking chairs. He tried to spit, but his mouth was dry as dust. Over and over, he moved the dirt around second base, smoothing out the area with his cleats while in between fielding a few practice grounders from first baseman Landy Colton. Right-handed pitcher Cody Hand threw his last warmup pitches before the seventh and final inning of the semi-final pony-league playoff game. The Tigers were in the heat of battle against the much-improved Pirates, with the winner moving on to the championship match to meet the undefeated Reds and their dominating pitcher Devlin King. Both the Tigers and the Pirates had lost two games during the regular season. The Tigers were now trying to hold on to a one-run lead as the Pirates had the meat of their lineup coming to bat.

TJ felt as though bees were flying around in his stomach. He chewed on the leather string on his new fielder's glove, hoping to calm his escalating nerves, which had reached an all-time high. Just two days earlier, TJ's mitt, well-oiled and broken into a comfortable softness like an old pair of tennis shoes, had suffered a tragedy. The family's new beagle puppy, Grounder, had snatched it from TJ's bedroom desk chair. He scrambled down the stairs past TJ and out the front door with the glove firmly between his teeth. TJ yelled at Grounder to stop, but he was outside and off to the races in seconds as TJ's mom had left the front door open to retrieve the mail. Grounder returned sometime later but without the glove. TJ and his mom looked everywhere. Later in the afternoon, when TJ's dad came home from work, the entire family searched around the house again. They looked in bushes, flowerbeds, behind garbage cans, under cars, and even gained permission from the next-door neighbors to check around their yards. They came up empty. TJ was devastated. He had played with the same glove for four years. It was only the second glove he had played with since tee-ball. With the playoff game just days away, TJ was gloveless. TJ's dad told him not to worry that he would buy him a new one. He told TJ that TJ had always taken care of his equipment, and it was just one of those zany things that happen sometimes. After visiting several sporting goods stores with his dad that same night, TJ finally settled on a small infielder's glove. It had that new glove stiffness but not as much as the others he tried on in each store. He was so used to his old glove it was just a part of him. The night he got his new glove, he took it home and gave it a good rubdown with some leather oil. He put an old baseball in the pocket, then wrapped several thick large rubber bands around the outside of the glove to keep it closed overnight. He then tucked it between some heavy books on an upper shelf in the bookcases in the den, high enough that Grounder could not reach it. All of this special treatment helped give it a little flexibility, and in a year or two, this new glove would be just as flexible as the one Grounder had taken away. However, the new glove was quite stiff, even with the oil treatment. Should the Tigers be fortunate enough to win, he would have to use it again in the championship.

With the hard-charging Pirates on the attack, the Pirates' leadoff hitter ripped the first pitch he saw from a tiring Cody into center field, followed by another hard shot into left field by the next batter. The runner from first base scampered all the way around to third. The tying run was one base away, and the winning run was now at first base with nobody out.

The Tigers' lead was in jeopardy, prompting Tigers' head coach Jack Parnell to call timeout and head to the mound to talk to his pitcher. With his tanned hands tucked away in the back of his uniform pants pockets and chewing on a large wad of Big-League Chew bubble gum, Coach P, as he was called, motioned for his catcher Diesel Jackson and all of his infielders to join him on the mound. Shortstop Wade Dadco, third baseman Scrap Wilson, first baseman Landy Colton and TJ gathered around their pitcher.

Coach P was only 24. He had played baseball since the age of seven and on through college. His playing days ended abruptly after hurting his throwing arm on a semi-pro team. Newly married with no children, he had received a call from an old family friend who was aware of Coach P's injury. The friend was now directing the community baseball association and asked if he would be interested in coaching a Pony League team of 13-14-year-old players. Coach P had never coached before, but he had tons of playing experience. The director told him they were having some difficulty filling the Tigers' coaching position with a qualified coach, and with his knowledge of the game, he would be a welcome addition. Coach P said it sounded fun, but he needed to talk to his wife and run it by her. Knowing how much her husband loved baseball and how busy she was with her job, she told him to go for it. He wasn't that much older than his players, but he knew the game. He had coached the Tigers to an outstanding record by teaching his players sound fundamentals. Now, here they were in a final playoff game trying to get to the championship.

The young Tigers' coach now stood on the mound studying his pitcher's face, gauging Cody's body language to calculate just how much gas his hurler had left in the tank.

In between blowing bubble after bubble, big ones, Coach P asked, “Do you have enough left to get through these next hitters, Cody?”

“Yes, sir,” the young pitcher weakly replied. Coach P looked at him carefully, uncertain if he was getting the truth. Cody realized quickly that Coach P wasn’t satisfied with his response.

“I can go, Coach,” he answered with a little more pep in his voice, stepping up his energy level. There was a lot on the line. He knew Coach P could pull him from the game if he thought Cody was not up to the task at hand. Rubbing his fingers across his chin, Coach P gave Cody an approving nod, and then looked at the other players standing on the hill.

“Okay. Here's what we are going to do." Turning his eyes to his catcher, he gave specific instructions. "Diesel, Cody is going to throw a fastball about a foot outside. When you catch it, you pretend to throw the ball to TJ at second base. The runner on first will be going on the pitch, I guarantee it. But you will have to sell it."

"What do you mean 'sell it,' Coach?" asked his catcher, a little confused.

"I mean, really act like you are trying to throw the runner out," Coach P replied. “Put a lot of arm and body motion into it, but instead of throwing it down to second base, you will keep the ball and then bring your arm down, still holding it by your side. As soon as you do that, Diesel, you will turn and throw the ball to third base, where Scrap will be moving in between third and the runner. It has to be quick with no delay."

“I don’t understand, Coach,” the Tigers’ third baseman said, totally confused.

“Everyone, listen to me closely,” Coach P said becoming a little frustrated. Trying hard to get his players to understand their roles in his strategy, he simplified his instructions. "In a nutshell, we are faking a throw to second and then quickly turning and throwing the ball to third base. When the runner on first base takes off for second base, and Diesel pretends to throw the ball to TJ, their third-base coach will send the runner at third, home," Coach P said as he slowly nodded over at the third-base coaching box.

"That's where you come in, Scrap. Play near the bag, but as soon as Cody delivers the pitch, you move between third and the runner. Diesel will throw it to you. Tag the runner or get him in a rundown. If he gets in a rundown, make him commit to a base and then make only one or two throws to get him out. We have practiced rundowns every practice. You guys know I don't like more than two throws in a rundown. Does everyone know what they are to do?"

"Ahh, Sweet, Coach!" Scrap said enthusiastically, finally grasping what it was he needed to do.

"What about me, Coach? Do I need to do anything?" asked Landy. Noticing the home plate umpire out of the corner of his eye heading to the mound to bring the meeting to a quick close, Coach P moved the conversation along rapidly.

"What are you supposed to do anytime you are playing first base and a runner tries to steal second?" Coach P asked her.

"I yell 'GOING!' Coach!"

"Exactly. The same applies here. That will also help sell our play."

"Got it, Coach P!" Landy replied. Landy was the only girl in the league and a better-than-average player.

"Let's go, guys, let's move the game forward," the umpire commanded. Coach P nodded and then gave his players a final bit of encouragement.

"All-hands, on deck! Now, make it work!" Coach P said, giving one last instruction and blowing one last big bubble as he clapped his hands and headed back to the dugout.

Cody went from the stretch on the rubber to hold the runners close to their bases. Diesel gave one finger down, then pointed to the outside of the plate, asking for a fastball. The right-handed hitter dug in. Cody delivered the pitch and the runner at first took off.

Landy yelled, "He's going!"

The pitch was a foot outside, and the batter swung and missed. Diesel came up out of his crouch and caught the fastball about chest high, which was in a perfect place to field and then throw. He fired such an impressive "fake" throw to second base that even Coach P thought his catcher had forgotten what he just directed to do and had actually thrown it. Still holding onto the baseball in his right hand, Diesel brought the ball back down to his right side just behind his hip as if he was Aaron Rodgers running the bootleg option. He then turned immediately towards third base, where he had just heard the third-base coach yell, "GO!" to the runner there.

The runner at third was racing towards home plate but then, realizing the Tigers' catcher still had the ball in his hands, immediately put the brakes on, looking like a deer in headlights. He turned to hustle back to third base, but Diesel's throw was right on the money to Scrap, who was standing just a few feet in front of the bag. Scrap made a swiping tag on the top of the runner's helmet as the fooled runner dove headfirst back to third.

"You're out!!" roared the third-base umpire with his right arm extended, pointing to the embarrassed runner who got up off the dirt, wiped off the front of his dirt-stained jersey, and with his head hanging low ambled back to his dugout.

"Nice work, Tigers!" Coach P shouted proudly to his team. They had just pulled off a brilliant defensive maneuver with some fine Oscar-worthy acting performances, especially by the heady catcher Diesel Jackson.

After tagging the runner at third, Scrap quickly turned and looked at second base, but the runner from first had reached there safely. Scrap had no other play. With the tying run now in scoring position at second base and one out, Cody had one strike on the batter. He was a stout kid who could pulverize the ball if he connected. Cody seemed energized now by the beautiful play he and his teammates had just pulled off. Maybe that boost would help him get through the rest of the lineup.

He swung at a fastball a foot outside, thought Cody. *I'll give him another one.*

Diesel called for a breaking ball, but Cody shook him off, wanting to throw a fastball instead. Again, the big hitter took a full swing at the pitch three inches off the outside corner and missed.

With two strikes on the hitter, Diesel now called for a fastball but Cody shook him off wanting to throw a slow curve. Cody's instincts were right again. The big slugger swung from his heels, missing the ball by two feet. In a big gamble, the runner at second stole third on the pitch. The good news is that now there were two outs. The bad news is the runner at third could now score not only on a base hit but also a wild pitch, passed ball, or a fielding error.

Cody needed to be extra careful here. Not only that, but the Pirates also had their cleanup hitter coming to the plate. One of the best hitters in the league, he had enough power to jack one out of the park. A big boy who loved hitting fastballs. Throw this guy a fastball too close to the middle of the plate, and it is *See Ya! Game Over*.

Cody knew he was gassed and was losing steam off of his fastball. He decided to throw breaking balls. He no longer had the strength in his arm to get fastballs past the big hitter. Cody shook off the sign for a fastball from Diesel and threw a curve instead. The Pirates slugger nearly came out of his big shoes trying to knock the slow, chest-high breaking pitch into another time zone. Instead, he fouled it behind the backstop.

Again, Diesel called for a breaking ball. Cody's pitch looked like it was heading straight for the slugger and, at the last second, broke beautifully over the inside corner for a called strike two with the batter offering no attempt at it. Nervous parents of both teams stood in their respective bleachers, closely watching the drama unfolding pitch by pitch. Those who had been sitting in lawn chairs around the park were now standing and rooting enthusiastically for their teams. Some of the moms bowed their heads, covering their eyes as they were too nervous to watch how this one was going to end.

Cody peered in for Diesel's signal. His catcher called for another curve, but something made Cody stop and back off the rubber. He thought about Diesel's pitch selection for a few seconds, then stepped back on the rubber, going from the stretch to keep the runner at third close to the bag in case there was a wild pitch or passed ball. Maybe they would have a shot at getting the runner if he didn't have a big lead.

Diesel put down two fingers for the curve. This time, however, Cody shook him off. Diesel looked out at his pitcher and put two fingers down again, only to be shaken off a second time. Surprised because the two breaking pitches had worked to perfection, Diesel gave in and put down one finger for the fastball. Cody nodded. He reached back, pulling up every ounce of strength he could muster, and delivered a fastball, trying to throw it past the big hitter. The slugger, expecting to see another slow curve, was shocked to see a fastball screaming towards the outside corner of the plate. Reacting quickly and at the last possible moment and through sheer strength, he was able to flick his wrists and get just enough of his big bat on the ball to produce a pop-up into shallow right field, just beyond first base and a few feet inside the right-field foul line. As much as the Tigers and their supporters were hoping for it to drift foul, this one was no doubt going to be landing in fair territory. The ball was looping straight for no-man's land, too far out of reach for Landy to turn at first base and run towards right field.

The Tigers' right fielder had been playing deep and towards center field, with the power-hitter up, so there was no way for him to make it in to make the play. The only one with any chance was TJ, who had been playing behind the second-base bag with the dead pull-hitter up. The guy was so strong he never hit the ball to the right side. However, this time, Cody had set him up with two slow curveballs and then surprised the hitter with a fastball on the corner that might have been called strike three had the hitter not made contact.

Since Abner Doubleday himself invented baseball, hundreds, no, thousands of games were determined by a batted ball either being a few inches fair or a few inches foul. Sometimes, just landing an inch away on either side of the chalk line or sometimes right on it. Freaky baseball luck. That's all it was. And now, it looked as though the

Tigers were going to have that freaky baseball luck go against them.

Cody had made the correct pitch. He had caught the hitter off guard. It was not a line drive blast into the outfield gaps or a power shot over the fence. This one was going to find a little patch of grass in fair territory just beyond the reach of the Tigers' defense. The Tigers' right fielder charged in hard, and Landy and TJ all broke immediately for the pop-up.

TJ was known as a superb defensive player. Although his hitting wasn't that strong, he was arguably the best defensive second baseman in the league. He was small in size but huge on heart and effort. As he made a beeline for the sinking looper, flashes of his dad throwing him high pop-ups in their spacious front yard at home ran through his mind.

"Make me dive, Dad!" and "Just one more," TJ would instruct his father as it became almost too dark to see on those wonderful father and son evenings of playing catch. What also ran through TJ's mind was that he had a stiff, new glove that he did not feel comfortable with, and how could he possibly make the catch. Not opening and closing it as effortlessly as he used to with his last glove could be a major problem. Even Grounder made a brief appearance in TJ's train of thoughts and not in a good way. *Why, Grounder? Why?* A lot was going on in TJ's head in those few seconds.

Still, TJ never took his eyes off of the rapidly descending baseball. He ran as hard as he could to try and get to that spot of outfield grass about ten yards beyond the dirt portion of the infield and first base where the ball was headed. The runner on third had reached home plate. The catch now had to be made, or the game would be tied.

Landy was getting close, but she had no chance. At the last possible second, TJ, still locked in and in a full-out sprint, stretched out his left arm, opening his glove. It wasn't easy. TJ's small hand struggled to open the new stiff mitt fully. The ball hit in the pocket, but because he was running so hard, he couldn't close his glove all the way, and the ball bounced out of the glove and up into the air. He lost his balance and fell to the ground, rolling over in a hard tumble.

Laying now on his back, he looked up and saw the ball dropping about three feet from him. He extended his glove as far as he could reach, with the back of the glove resting on the ground. The ball plopped dead solid into the pocket. TJ didn't move a muscle as he was afraid the slightest movement would cause the ball to come loose. What seemed like an eternity abruptly ended when he looked up and saw the first-base umpire who had run out towards shallow right field standing over him. After seeing that TJ had the baseball secured, he lifted his fist into the air and yelled loudly enough for everyone in the entire ballpark to hear, "Out! Ball game!"

Delirious with joy, TJ's teammates ran out to him and began piling on their second baseman, knocking him back down to the grass. TJ disappeared under the stack of Tigers, which was growing higher by the second. They threw gloves as high as they could into the night sky, giving each other hugs, shouting, "We're going to the championship!"

"Great catch, TJ!" added Cody.

"That catch will be on ESPN tonight!" proclaimed Scrap.

The parents and fans of the Tigers poured out from the bleachers and their lawn chairs, high-fiving one other as they made their way inside the fence and onto the field to take pictures and be a part of the jubilant celebration. They were congratulated by a few of the sad but gracious in defeat Pirates' fans, saying "Outstanding catch" and "Never seen a better play out here."

Coach P and his two assistant coaches, all sporting big grins, gave each other bear hugs but realized their second baseman was at the bottom of a large pile of players and needed air hustled out to pull him to safety. Dazed and out of breath from being crushed, TJ sported a grin from ear to ear. As cameras clicked away, he held the ball high over his head for all to see. The Tigers on their way to the championship game.

2

Devlin King was the tallest, rudest, and cockiest kid in Ashford Park Middle School. He was also the best baseball player in the local pony league and most likely the entire state for his age group. A 14-year-old with straggly blonde hair that fell to his shoulders, Devlin stood six feet, four inches tall, towering over all of the kids in the school. He was the king in his middle school, where he walked the hallways with a swagger. No one dared challenge him. Those who witnessed Devlin fight saw him end those fights quickly and without mercy. The combination of his nastiness and size made him unbeatable. No one looked to fight Devlin anymore as his reputation had been well established for some time.

On the other hand, life at home presented other issues for him. Much of the time, his parents frequently argued in front of Devlin and his younger brother and sister. Unfortunately, many of Devlin's character traits likely came from Devlin's father. The lousy character traits. Devlin could never please him even after playing a great game. He could hit two homers, knock in five runs, pitch a one-hit shutout, but on the way home from the game, would be criticized and berated by his father for not throwing a no-hitter. Still, with all the problems Devlin encountered at home, he thrived on the diamond and dominated on the hill. He gained much enjoyment from staring down batters, many of whom were half his size. His wiry, muscular build and his physical appearance were intimidating. His steely gray eyes were hard to see from the batter's box because he pulled the bill of his hat down and squinted, not because he had poor eyesight, he just wanted to look scary to hitters.

Devlin's scorching fastball was epic. Very few hitters in the league could solidly connect with it. For the most part, he had control of his pitches, but once in a while one would get away from him, nailing a hitter. Batters would feel the sting from one of Devlin's fastballs for days. Most of the time those pitches that got away from him were purely accidental but there were those occasions his wild pitches were intentional. He was just plain mean.

Devlin would purposely hit a batter if he thought they were hitting him more than they should or if he just didn't like them. Most of the time, when batters picked up his fastball, it was usually in the catcher's mitt. He was the hardest throwing pitcher this league had ever seen. He was, as they say, "The King of the Hill."

3

The lunchroom at Ashford Park Middle School was bustling and quite loud this Friday, the final day of the school year. Testing was over, the weather was warming up, and there would be no more homework or fussy teachers to deal with for the next ten weeks. Summer vacation would begin in a few hours. The teams for the league championship were set, and the game would be played in just eight days. The Tigers would square off against the undefeated Reds and Devlin King.

“Hey Scrap, do you think we have a chance to win next Saturday?” Landy asked him as they walked through the lunch line checking out the unappealing food offerings.

"Well, we know who's pitching for them, so our chances are slim to none, and Slim just left town," said Scrap, grinning, proud of his joke.

“What do you mean, Slim left town? Oh, I get it," she said, shaking her head at Scrap. Where did you come up with that one?” she asked.

“It’s just who I am, L!" laughed Scrap. "I'm not only good-looking, but I’m also brilliant and witty as all get out!”

Landy was the lone girl in the entire league, a left-handed hitter and fielder with lots of athletic ability. Her girlfriends wanted her to play in the softball league with them, but Landy had played baseball with her older brother and his buddies in neighborhood pickup games since she was six years old. Anytime they were short a player, she became the go-to add-on. She liked softball and missed playing with her girlfriends, but she loved baseball—real hardball with overhand pitching.

Landy also always felt she was as good as boys in baseball, and she had something to prove. When she would hear folks say that a girl should be playing softball or soccer and leave baseball to the boys, it only fueled her desire to show further what she could do. And not just with sports. Nothing could rile her more than someone telling her there was something she couldn't do, for whatever reason.

She wanted to play quarterback on the 12-and-under Pop Warner football team, and the only reason she didn't was that her dad stepped in and said," absolutely not!" She argued and pleaded her case over and over but to no avail. This one, her dad would not budge in his decision. Too dangerous. To his credit, he would not allow his son to play either. Many of the dads coaching football he had noticed did not know proper ways to teach blocking and tackling. In reality, Landy's dad had told her mom that "Landy is my little girl and always will be. No way is she playing tackle football."

She was also a starting forward on the middle-school girls' basketball team who could shoot the lights out from the corner. Her tall thin frame with excellent hands also afforded her above-average skills as a first baseman. She could hold her own with the boys in the pony league, was a productive hitter, and was keenly aware of what was going on every minute of the game on the field. Although it took a few practices and a couple of games for the boys on the team to accept her, she proved herself to be a valuable player, and was now totally embraced by her teammates.

"I think we can win," interjected TJ as he overheard his teammates in the lunch line. That comment brought a few quizzical looks on some of the faces, questioning whether TJ had lost his senses.

"I know, I know," said TJ, seeing the doubt circulating among the group. "King is pitching, but we have a good team, or we wouldn't be in the championship."

"Are you crazy, TJ?" Scrap retorted with a sour face, putting three cartons of chocolate milk on his lunch tray. The man is unhittable. He owns the hill, dude! You should know that as well as anyone, TJ," Scrap said, rubbing it in TJ's face that he could never hit King.

Ouch! That hurt, TJ thought, really getting his feelings shattered with that zinger.

"Scrap. Does your big mouth ever stop moving?" Landy barked, defending TJ. Like most of the other players in the league, TJ had suffered greatly at the plate against Devlin King. He had faced King four times the previous season. The results: No hits, three strikeouts, one walk.

He was almost the complete opposite of Devlin King. TJ was one of the smallest kids in the league, while Devlin was the tallest. TJ possessed no hitting power and was more of a singles hitter while Devlin could hit with tons of power. TJ was liked by just about everyone who knew him. Devlin King was "liked" only by some, primarily because they were afraid NOT to like him. TJ lived and breathed baseball. Outside of his schoolwork, chores, and playing ball with his friends, he would check in on ESPN during baseball season to see how his favorite team, the Atlanta Braves, and his favorite player, Dansby Swanson fared the night before. TJ even wore the number 7 on his jersey, just like his baseball hero.

When his dad was away on business, TJ would take a hard rubber-coated baseball and throw it against a four-foot-high, concrete wall that framed the backside of their patio in the backyard. He would take a piece of chalk, outline a square about 12 inches by 12 inches on the wall, making a target to improve his accuracy with his throws. He always started from about 50 feet away and gradually would move up to within six feet of the wall for his last throws. By throwing the rubber ball at the base of the wall where the ground and wall met, TJ could make the ball move to imitate line drives and pop-ups. Being so close helped him improve his reaction time. Practicing like this gave him superb fielding skills. If TJ had any alone time, the wall is where you could find him. He would practice for hours until his mom would call him in to supper.

Not the type of kid that someone would look at and think he was very athletic, TJ, although slight in stature, could make unreal plays with his glove. Possessing very soft hands, a great asset, especially for middle infielders, just made him even better defensively. He also had baseball intuition. He had a strong sense of where batters would hit a pitch. The majority of the time, TJ was right.

The other baseball skill TJ had developed over the last couple of years was laying down bunts. He had become Coach P's most reliable bunter. He took pride in this skill and was willing to sacrifice himself for the team's good to move runners around on the bases.

"You know, Scrap, there are other ways to win a baseball game," TJ said with a tinge of anger in his voice, upset that Scrap had said something so hurtful to him.

"I know that, bro. No problem," Scrap replied, now feeling a little guilty about hurting his teammate's feelings. "I just meant Devlin is unbeatable, and you would understand we don't have a shot. That's all," Scrap replied.

"By the way, how many hits do you have off of King?" TJ asked Scrap.

"Well, I will have to think on that one," Scrap replied but knowing full well he only had one hit, and that was a slow roller that the third baseman could not get to in time to throw Scrap out at first. Scrap beat the throw by a step. That was his hit. "Let's see. There was a game last year. Now, how many times did I come up against King? Uhmmm..."

“Why do you have to think about it, moron?" Landy interrupted Scrap as he pretended to calculate the number of his hits against Devlin. "Do you have so many you can't keep count?"

“Well,” Scrap shot back.

“Well, what?” Landy replied, pushing Scrap for a response.

“Well, I have at least one more than TJ!” snapped Scrap.

TJ was just about to reply to Scrap’s biting remark but remained quiet, deciding to just keep his comment inside. It wasn’t going to be worth it. There would be another time and place.

Scrap was two months shy of turning 14 but could often act like he was 6 or 40. He could be a brat or a fierce mature competitor and protector. He was short and somewhat stocky in build, sporting a crew-cut hairstyle similar to those haircuts new marines receive at basic training. He was tagged with "Scrap" when he was about five years old. There were many times when Scrap would come in from playing outside somewhat scraped and dirtied from being in a scrap or tussle with some of the kids in the neighborhood. It didn't matter if his foes were older, larger, or stronger than him. Nothing stopped Scrap from running his mouth, and before he knew it, he was rolling on the ground wrestling. He wore the bruises he would receive in battle as badges of honor, and he never shied away from embellishing the story behind each of those scuffles.

Scrap was a loyal friend to all who knew him, though. He could be hilarious as he was always cracking his teammates up in the dugout with made-up stories, silly jokes, or imitating someone. He especially loved to perform impressions of his friends, umpires, and teachers when they weren't watching.

TJ and Scrap were close pals. They could give each other a few shots here and there, but Landy was another matter. Scrap could not get away with much if she were around. She loved Scrap like a brother, but he could get under her skin, just like he could with everybody.

As they found a few empty seats at the lunch table next to some of their Tigers' teammates, they looked down the length of the lunch table to the far end and noticed the king holding court with a few members of the Reds.

"Well, I'm not worried about the championship game," boasted Devlin purposely loud enough for the Tigers and many of those seated in the cafeteria to hear. "Why should I be. Who are we playing? I don't know and don't care. Oh yeah, we are playing the Dirt-Wad Sissies, I think. If the Dirt-Wad Sissies get one hit off of me, it will be a miracle."

Devlin cut his eyes over at the Tigers to see their reaction. The Tigers sat there and said nothing. They knew that's how Devlin King operated, and none of them wanted to get into a confrontation with him. All, that is, except one. Scrap. He was not going to allow Devlin to get away with saying what he just said.

Scrap pushed his folding chair away from the table and stepped upon it. Now standing erect and looking straight ahead over his audience, not at anybody or anything, in particular, prompting his tablemates to stop eating and look up at him, all wondering what he was about to do next. There was no telling with Scrap. He began one of the many impressions he had performed over the last couple of years of Devlin.

"If the QUEEN of the hill strikes me out even one time it will be a miracle. Yes, I'm that good," said Scrap boldly. Scrap then nonchalantly stepped down off his chair, trying to keep from laughing at himself for his impression of Devlin.

Devlin glared over at Scrap, stood up abruptly, grabbed the back of his chair, and slung it down the row behind everyone's chairs towards his nemesis. The metal chair just missed Scrap's chair, which prompted the noisy lunchroom to become very quiet.

"Queen of the hill? You got a problem, stubby?" Devlin asked as he walked towards Scrap.

"Just one. Thanks for asking. I have a pain in my butt, and it seems to be coming from your direction."

Devlin now stood over Scrap, staring down at him in his lunchroom chair. Scrap realized at that point he had made Devlin very angry. One of the hazards of Scrap running his mouth was that he didn't thoroughly think through the impact of his words and comments. Devlin leaned over while pressing his hand down hard on Scrap's shoulder.

"You never know when a pitch might get away from me, Crap Head!" Devlin whispered, issuing a stern warning to Scrap. "If I, were you, I wouldn't stand too close to the plate when you come up to bat," warned Devlin.

"Yep. I know your control is ridiculous," Scrap said with fake enthusiasm. "Ridiculously rotten is how I would describe it."

That prompted more laughter from those nearby.

"Oh really?" Devlin replied. "If my control is so rotten, then why does everyone call me the king of the hill?"

"Not sure why they call you that name. Oh, wait a minute. I know why they call you king of the hill. Because you have a throne," Scrap said, looking up at Devlin without skipping a beat. "And by the throne, I mean the toilet! And say, why don't you go sit on it right now?" Scrap said while pointing to the boys' restroom on the other side of the cafeteria.

All of the Tigers and even some of the Reds at their table broke up laughing. King turned and glared at his tablemates, which caused them to clam up instantly. *How dare his teammates laugh at a joke on him*? Devlin grabbed Scrap by the collar on the back of his shirt and began lifting him out of his chair when Ms. James, the 8th-grade science teacher who had noticed the activity, rose from her lunch table where she was sitting with some of the other teachers and hurried over.

"Mr. King! Young man, return to your table, pick up your tray and turn it in. You are finished eating!" she stated in a stern voice.

"But I...I...I..." stammered Devlin.

"You are done!" she said, raising her voice and offering Devlin an icy stare. As he left his table with half a tray of uneaten food left on it, Devlin turned and walked back towards Scrap.

"We'll finish this later," whispered Devlin as he walked by Scrap and allowed his right elbow to firmly greet the back of Scrap's head.

"You better be careful, Scrap," TJ warned. "You got under his skin, big time."

Scrap grinned and cockily replied, "Just what I was trying to do. Throw him off his game. He will be so mad at us and jacked up next week he will throw nothing but balls. He will walk all of us, and we'll win the championship."

"Yeah, and monkeys might fly out of my butt," quipped Landy, prompting a roar of laughter from those nearby.

"I hope you know what you are doing, Scrap," TJ said, a little concerned. "He's pretty mad."

The group noticed Ms. James following Devlin to the tray return area. She had him in her sights and was moving in fast.

"Devlin. Did I just see you hit Scrap with your elbow?" she asked, approaching him a second time. Devlin quickly thought about it and knew the right thing to say but just could not bring himself to get the words out.

"No," Devlin mumbled, turning his head away from her to avoid eye contact.

"I know what I saw," Ms. James replied. She had done her best to get through this final day of the school year with no issues, but she did not tolerate bad behavior in her classroom or anywhere else, for that matter. Even more so, Ms. James did not put up with lying, which is just what Devlin did. She spoke briefly with Devlin's teacher at another table and then turned towards Devlin.

"Follow me," she commanded, wiggling her index finger at him. Everyone in the lunchroom watched as Ms. James led Devin out into the hallway. It was apparent they were headed straight for the principal's office.

"Hey, Scrap," Landy said as they watched Ms. James escort Devlin out of the lunchroom. "Have you ever heard of something called karma?"

"Yep, sure have. It's supposedly some really bad stuff; Voodoo, black magic, or something. So what? I don't believe in that crazy weird crap," Scrap replied, shrugging off Landy's question.

"Karma doesn't always have to be bad," Landy replied. "What you send out into the world comes back to you the same way you send it out. If you do something friendly or positive, something nice or positive comes back to you. That's called good karma. But if you do evil, negative stuff, then that is what might come back on you. Bad karma. You might have just put out a little bad karma with Devlin."

"Well, I think I just put out good karma, L," Scrap replied. "Devlin is the devil, and I just got the devil in trouble. That's good stuff, right?" he said as he performed a hand drum roll on the cafeteria table for entertainment value.

"Hey! I can't go to the movies in the morning," Landy said, changing the subject.

"How come?" asked TJ.

"I'm going out of town for the weekend to see my grandparents," she replied." "My grandfather is not doing well. They may not be able to come to the championship game so my mom said we need to go see them now."

"How long will you be gone?" Scrap asked.

"Well, I have to be back for practice on Monday afternoon, so we will be back before then. Could be just about the time practice starts, though."

"Man, I wanted to see King Kong again," said a disappointed Scrap. "It's my all-time favorite movie."

"So, how many times have you seen it?" Landy asked, knowing he had seen it a lot.

"Five times now," Scrap boasted.

"It's ok," said TJ. "We can wait until next week, Landy. Scrap will have to wait a few days to see number six."

A few minutes later, TJ and Scrap left the cafeteria together with their classmates to return to their classroom when they noticed Devlin sitting in the office near the secretary's desk. He was by himself and appeared to be very agitated. As TJ and Scrap walked by the office, Devlin pointed at Scrap and slowly mouthed the words, "I'll get you for this."

"I told you he was angry," TJ said.

Scrap did not respond to TJ but shot a glance or two over his shoulder at Devlin as he made his way to his classroom. It wasn't much later that word had traveled throughout the school that Devlin's parents had come and met with the principal. Devlin had to clean out his locker and leave the school. He had been suspended for the rest of the day, even though there were only a few hours left in the school year.

When Landy heard the news, she couldn't wait to see Scrap in the hallway during the next change of classes, delighted with the prospect that Devlin might also have to miss the big game.

"I just heard Devlin got suspended. He may not be able to play in the championship either," she told Scrap excitedly as they stood by Scrap's locker. She couldn't remember if it was a league rule, but she remembered a player having to miss some games because of a similar situation.

"Well, we might have a shot now, L," Scrap replied, thrilled with the thought of Devlin not being on the mound for the big one and more excited about the possibility that Devlin would not be able to give Scrap a little payback. "Looks like that good karma is beginning to take hold."

"By the way, Scrap, your locker is a mess," Landy said, ignoring his comment about karma as she looked over the mayhem of notebooks, food, and candy wrappers strewn about. Scrap's locker was a lot like him, total chaos.

"It's the last day of school; what do I care?" Scrap replied with total indifference. Landy shook her head and walked away but her thoughts quickly turned to her grandfather.

4

Landy was very close to her grandfather. They talked baseball every time they were together. He spent a few years playing semi-pro but never made it to the majors. The first thing he would always ask after a quick hello hug during baseball season was, "How is your team doing?" She still held out hope he would be able to come to see her play in the championship game, even though he was very ill. She knew he wanted to see her play again more than anything in the world.

With the family car gassed up and packed, Landy's family took off for the small town in Alabama where her mother's folks lived right after school let out on Friday afternoon. She had dressed in her baseball uniform minus the cleats as she always did when seeing her grandfather. He loved seeing her in her "uni."

The last two hours of the five-hour trip, with the car windows down and some cool night air blowing in, Landy slept peacefully in the backseat with her older brother. Upon arriving, she gave her grandmother a big hug and immediately went to her grandfather's room. He was lying in his bed, weak and pale from battling cancer.

For the first time she could see how sick her grandfather was. She had not known how bad his condition was as her parents did not want to upset her and her brother with the last days of school and final testing. Her grandfather opened his arms and received her hug as she leaned over his bed.

"We are in the championship next weekend Grand Dad. I hope you can come," Landy said, struggling to say each word as she looked down upon her grandfather's pale face. He gave her a little wink but didn't speak at all. As long as she could remember, that had never happened before. She knew then he would not be making the trip to see her play in the championship.

After a couple of minutes, Landy's mom held her hand and led her out of the room, closing the door behind them. Landy broke into tears and fell into her mom's arms. They went into a guest bedroom and sat down on the bed, her mom holding her. No words were spoken. After just a few minutes of crying into her mom's shoulder, Landy fell onto her bed and quickly went to sleep.

Landy awoke late Saturday morning to the news her grandfather had passed away sometime during the night. At one point in the day's early hours, she had heard talking in hushed tones as s well as some movement throughout the house but then fell back asleep.

After breakfast, Landy and her brother sat on the front porch swing remembering their grandfather and the funny things he would say and do. They talked about the first time he took them fishing. He had started them out with just a small Charlie Brown and Snoopy rod and reel with some live red worms for bait.

"Remember when I caught that huge catfish as soon as I cast my line in the water?" Landy asked her brother.

"Yep, that was crazy," he said with a laugh. "He had to stop putting the worm on my hook to help you pull the catfish onto the bank."

“That thing nearly pulled me in the water,” she said. "I was only seven."

Great memories. Now, Landy's grandfather was gone. Landy's mom told her the last words he spoke were, "Get Landy to her game." Upon hearing those words, Landy cried again.

5

TJ answered a knock at the door late Saturday afternoon. A Hispanic boy TJ did not recognize and about TJ's age, but a tad taller stood shyly on the front porch holding what appeared to be a very worn and wet piece of leather.

"Is this your glove?" the young visitor asked with a friendly smile and slight accent.

“Oh wow!” replied TJ. “Yes. That’s it! My dog took off with it last week. We looked all over for it. Where did you find it?”

"We just moved in and found it under our deck in the backyard. I asked your neighbor next door if it belonged to them, and they said you had lost a glove," said the boy. Ragged and still wet from the rains and Grounder’s chewing, the glove was now a soggy mess.

“Thanks for bringing it over,” TJ said with a half-smile while looking over its poor condition. “My dad had to buy me a new one. What’s your name?”

“Alejandro.”

"I'm TJ. Want to come in?"

"Sure, if it's okay," Alejandro replied.

TJ introduced Alejandro to his mom, telling her about Alejandro moving across the street and finding the glove under their deck.

"Thank you, Alejandro. We all looked hard for that glove but never thought to look under there,” TJ's mom said.

“What is your last name?” she asked.

“Garcia,” he replied.

“Well, I will go over and introduce myself to your mother. Is she home, now?”

"No. She took my sisters shopping. She should be home soon, though."

"Okay, I'll go over a little later. Thanks again for bringing the glove, or what’s left of it. And, by the way, that little beast right there is the one who took it over to your house," TJ's mom said, pointing at Grounder, who sat quietly on the couch, trying not to look guilty, knowing the evidence had been returned.

"He's cute," Alejandro said as he knelt to pet him. Grounder not only allowed Alejandro to do so but rolled over for a belly rub.

“Where did the name Grounder come from?” Alejandro asked TJ.

“My mom and dad said I could keep him after I found him wandering in the woods one day. I love fielding ground balls so I named him Grounder, you know, baseball stuff.”

TJ escorted Alejandro upstairs to TJ's room, where TJ sat on his bed, and Alejandro sat in the desk chair. The same desk chair Grounder had pulled the glove off.

“Do you play on a baseball team, TJ?”

“Yep. The Tigers. We have a championship game coming up next weekend. It is the end of the season. Last game. Do you play?”

"Si," answered Alejandro as he glanced around the room at all of the baseball posters of major league players on TJ's walls. "We just moved to Georgia from Texas. I played on a team there but had to stop before the season ended because my father transferred here with his job. I was going to see if I could play on a team here, but I guess it is too late," Alejandro said with noticeable disappointment.

"What league did you play in Texas?"

“I played pony league.”

"That's our league here, thirteen and fourteen-year-old league," TJ replied. "How old are you?"

"I'm fourteen. I just had my birthday the day we left Texas."

“Were you able to have a party?” TJ asked.

"Sort of. A few friends came over to say goodbye the night before we left. We had some cake, but that was about it. Is this a good neighborhood TJ? Are there a lot of kids our age living here?”

“Yep. There are a bunch. So, you will go to the same high school next year with me, right?” TJ asked.

"Si. We wanted to move here during the summer so my brothers and sisters and I could be settled before school starts in August. Maybe meet new friends too."

TJ could tell as soon as Alejandro spoke on the front porch, not only did TJ like him, he knew they would be good friends. TJ just had that vibe, just like the gut feeling of knowing where ground balls would be hit during ball games.

“How many brothers and sisters do you have?” TJ asked.

"Two brothers, both older than me, and two sisters. They are younger than me," Alejandro replied. "They all play soccer. I am the only one who plays baseball. It is my favorite sport. My favorite player is Mike Trout of the Angels. Who is yours?”

“Dansby Swanson of the Braves,” TJ replied, pointing to a large poster of the Braves’ great shortstop taped on the wall over his bed.

"I like Dansby, too. We follow the Braves a lot because we got all their games on TV," Alejandro replied.

“What position do you play?” TJ asked his new friend.

"I'm a shortstop. I've played a lot of other positions, but shortstop is my favorite.”

“I play second base,” TJ said. “Hey, maybe next year we can be on the same team and be a great middle-infield duo.”

“That would be cool,” Alejandro replied. “Do they have a JV team?"

"Yep. It is tough to make it because there are a lot of good players around," TJ said. "Not impossible, though. The best pitcher probably in the entire state is in our league and will go to the same high school next year. His name is Devlin King. He throws faster than any of the seniors on the high school team right now, and he is an eighth-grader. He will be on the varsity team, and even though he will be a freshman, he will probably be the number one pitcher. Everybody says he will sign a professional baseball contract as soon as he graduates. He's tall, and he is very mean. If he doesn't like you, he might throw one at you. We are playing his team Saturday. The Reds. They haven't lost a game all year. Not even close. He will pitch for them, so we don't have much of a chance. He got in trouble on the last day of school and was suspended for the rest of the day. We are all hoping he will have to miss the championship game, but no one knows for sure what the league will do."

"Oh, man. This King guy sounds rough," Alejandro said, raising his eyebrows.

"That's a definite yes," replied TJ. "We call him the king of the hill because he's such a dominating pitcher. I guess you could say he owns the mound. Well, I say we call him the king of the hill. He calls himself that. No one has ever beaten him. He's a great hitter, too. He has hit more home runs than anyone in the league."

"I think I should try and stay away from such a person," Alejandro replied.

"You would be wise to stay away. That's what I do. Or at least I try. Would you like to come to the championship game with us Saturday? You would be able to see where we play and meet some of my teammates, too."

"I'll check with my mom, but I'd like to come, for sure," Alejandro said, happy that finding TJ's glove under his backyard deck led him to also find his first friend in the neighborhood.

6

On Monday morning, TJ ate breakfast and called Scrap on his cell phone waking him up.

"Have you heard anything yet about Devlin?" TJ asked.

"The only thing I heard was that his parents were at first really upset with the principal and Ms. James, but when they got Devlin home, they punished him pretty badly, Scrap replied with a big yawn. Not sure what that means, though."

"Who did you hear that from?" TJ asked.

"My aunt lives next door to Devlin," replied Scrap.

"Man, that would be awesome if Devlin had to sit the championship out," TJ replied. "You did a good job of getting him in trouble."

"Hey, I wasn't trying to get him in trouble. He just really brings out my bad side," Scrap said.

"Well, for what it's worth, it paid off," TJ said. "I guess we'll see, anyway.
Is Landy back from her grandparents?"

"I don't think so," Scrap replied. "I haven't heard from her."

"Don't think we are practicing today or maybe tomorrow either," said TJ. "Been raining all night and supposed to, today and tomorrow."

"Well, that stinks," Scrap replied as he walked over to his bedroom window to confirm TJ's weather report.

“My mom just called me. I gotta go," said TJ. "Call me later if you find out anything on Landy."

“Will do,” Scrap replied.

For three days, heavy rains soaked the area. All practices for both teams were canceled. TJ could not work out the stiffness of his new glove other than just sitting around the house flexing it on his hand. On Wednesday evening, the skies finally cleared, and the forecast was beautiful weather for the next five days, which would cover the championship on Saturday night. Thursday morning, Landy finally reached out to Scrap on the phone.

“Hey,” she said to Scrap in a monotone voice.

"Okay, what's wrong?" Scrap asked her.

“What do you mean?” she replied quietly.

"You never just say 'hey to me. You usually call me a moron or something.”

“My grandfather passed away last weekend. The funeral was yesterday,” Landy said as she began to cry softly.

“I’m really sorry, L,” Scrap replied with unexpected sincerity.

“How are practices going?” she asked, with little enthusiasm. She wanted to talk about something else. Every time she tried to talk about her grandfather, she became emotional.

"We haven't even been able to go outside all week because of all the rain we have had," Scrap said. "The fields are too wet to practice on, so Coach P said we would get together at the field this afternoon just to throw. We will hopefully have a full practice tomorrow afternoon."

"What's the latest with Devlin?" Landy asked.

"My aunt heard he got in big trouble with his parents, but that's all we know," Scrap said. "No one has seen him around."

"Too bad," Landy replied. "I will be there today," she said, but sounding as if she really didn't care one way or another about playing baseball.

"Really? Awesome!" Scrap said cheerfully, excited that his friend was coming home.

"We are about to leave. I'll see you later at practice," Landy replied.

Scrap knew Landy was not herself and that losing her grandfather was tough for her. But he also decided he would try and cheer her up the best he could. Even though Scrap always seemed to be on the receiving end of Landy's verbal shots, he thought a lot of her. Landy also thought a lot of Scrap, just like a brother, if truth be told.

7

The Tigers showed up for their 4 p.m. throwing practice on Thursday, stunned at how wet the fields were. The Reds would be able to use the field at 6:15 p.m. Nobody would be doing anything except loosening their arms because of the multitude of large puddles of water in the infield and outfield. The hitting cages down the foul lines outside the field were also engulfed in standing water.

“Oh man, the field is a lake. How can we play on this?” Scrap shouted to his teammates as they paired up in right field and threw to each other. All except Cody. He told Coach P that he did not want to throw as soon as he arrived. His arm was still worn out from pitching the entire playoff game. Cody and Reno Ivey were the best pitchers on the team. Throwing anyone else against the Reds would be giving the game away. With Cody and Reno, the Tigers had a chance, although a very small one. Both Cody and Reno were real pitchers who knew how to use their breaking pitches and locate a fastball. Now, all Coach P could do after hearing that Cody's arm was shot was to come to the realization Reno was the man who would have to go all the way in the championship unless the game just got out of hand, then it wouldn’t matter.

“Coach P said they have a lot of volunteers coming tomorrow to work the field and that the sun will help dry up a lot of the water," said Billy.

“Hey, L," Scrap yelled out to Landy while throwing with TJ, trying to engage her and cheer her up. "It was raining like cats and dogs here this week. I almost stepped in a poodle. Get it? A poodle?"

Landy just stared at Scrap, who then felt the need to explain his joke.

"You know, like a puddle except it was a poodle because of the 'cats and dogs."

No one laughed.

"Somebody put me out of my misery right now," said Diesel, who suddenly broke out in laughter as Scrap's corny joke finally registered with him. Several more teammates also followed Diesel and began to laugh hysterically. Being cooped up most of the week from the rains had kept everyone's emotions locked up as well. Now they could all breathe a little bit and let off some steam. Almost all were laughing except Landy. She didn't break a smile. Coach P monitoring the throwing could tell his first baseman was hurting from losing her grandfather. Landy was grieving in a major way. Wade, standing near Scrap, threw his glove at him and called Scrap a Ninny.

"What's a Ninny?" TJ asked Wade.

"I'm not sure, but that name just fits him," said Wade, laughing. Scrap ran over to Wade, looked him square in the face, and started making sounds like a goat.

"That's a Ninny, Dadco!" Scrap explained as he jabbed his finger into Wade's chest. That set Wade off. He took off after Scrap chasing him around the wet outfield.

Just as Wade was gaining on Scrap, Wade's right foot and ankle disappeared into a large hole in the ground filled with water, causing a nasty twist of his right knee. Wade fell over immediately onto the ground, grabbing his knee with both hands, his eyes filling with tears because of the intense pain. Coach P, who had been watching it all unfold, hustled out to his injured shortstop. Scrap, realizing that Wade was hurt, ran back to his teammate. The other coaches and players all gathered around in quick order.

"He's really hurting," Coach P said with great concern. "His parents aren't here, and I'm afraid to move him."

One of the assistant coaches called 911, and an ambulance arrived within twenty minutes to take Wade to the hospital. Wade's parents were called and told to meet the ambulance there. Coach P gave a disappointing look at his assistant coaches. They all knew Wade would not be playing in the championship game in two days.

The atmosphere took a somber tone as the team walked around in stunned silence, basically for the rest of their throwing session, which would now be shortened due to the time spent on the entire event. Close to an hour had been lost from attending to Wade and waiting on the ambulance.

Coach P took the team into the dugout with a few minutes left in practice and spoke about focusing on practice and games.

"I know that you guys have been locked up for a while because of the rain. But you see that when you horse around, accidents can happen. I know, Scrap, you didn't mean for Wade to get injured. I know that you wish you had it to do over again. Wade is at fault too. We just have to be more mindful of what we are supposed to be doing. Keep that in mind for the next few days. Now, the other coaches and I have to figure out who will play shortstop. Go home, get some rest and be ready to practice at 1 p.m. tomorrow. We will need All Hands-on Deck now, for sure," Coach P finished up.

Scrap felt terrible. They could not afford to lose one of the best players on the team with the championship on the line coming up. As Coach P and his coaches stepped away from the players as they collected their equipment bags and departed for home quietly and with sad faces, TJ walked over to where the coaches were huddling.

"Coach P, I might have someone who can play shortstop for us. A kid just moved into the house across the street from me. He played pony league in Texas. He's a shortstop."

"Do you know if he is any good, TJ?"

"I don't know, Coach P. I really just met him."

"I will have to check on the league rules, TJ. I will check with Wade's parents tonight. We will see what the doctor says. I will let you know either way, but it could be late tonight before I call you. I am not sure if the league will allow a new player with only the championship left, but we'll see. Please don't say anything to your friend about this yet. I don't want to get his hopes up, and then the league says he can't play, okay?"

“Okay, Coach.”

After TJ left the field, coach P resumed his conversation with his two coaches.

"I didn't want to say anything in front of TJ, but we are next on the list to add a player if we lose one. Remember, we had one less player than the other teams at the start of the season except for the Dodgers, and they picked up a new player that moved into the area the second or third game of the season. We are next to add one. I will push for this. It shouldn't make a difference if there are ten games left to play or one game left. Let's hold out hope Wade can play but based upon what I just saw, he is finished for the year. He's a tough kid, but I can't picture him playing. If he can't play, then let's all hope there is a better than average player on the waiting list, or at least this friend of TJ's is a decent shortstop. We can play Cody there, but I want to keep him rested if we need him to throw a few innings in relief. Let's try to think positively. At our absolute best, it would be extremely tough with Devlin on the mound. Now, we will just have to play the cards dealt to us."

Coach P called Wade's mother later that night to find out any update on his condition. She said the doctor had examined him and had determined Wade had a tear in his ACL, which would require surgery. Wade’s season was over. Coach P said he was sorry and said he would drop by the next day to check on him. He then called the league director and informed him of the situation. He told the director the Tigers were next on the list to add a player since they were the only team with eleven players when the others all had twelve. He also reminded the director that the Dodgers, the other team with eleven, had replaced their player early in the season, and now it was their turn. Coach P then questioned the director about the school suspension for Devlin and asked if he would be allowed to play in the championship.

The director said there were no official league rules, but it was up to the Reds head coach to decide. When the director asked the Reds coach if he was going to further punish Devlin by not allowing him to play, the coach said it wouldn't be fair for Devlin to have played the entire season and then have to miss the championship because of something that had happened the last few hours at school. The league director felt the same way but said the overriding decision for him was that Devlin's home life was so bad he just didn't have the heart to keep him from playing. That move could cause an already troubled young man to become even more troubled.

Coach P knew this would be the case before he ever asked the question.

After Coach P received approval from the director to add a player, he called TJ, told him about Wade, and asked if he had Alejandro's phone number. TJ said he would get it for him asap and then call Coach P back.

TJ was excited as he ran out the front door to Alejandro's house across the street and knocked on the front door. Alejandro answered and saw TJ sporting a big grin.

"How would you like to play in our game this Saturday?" TJ asked his new friend.

"How can I do that? I'm not on the team," replied Alejandro.

"Our shortstop got hurt at practice. My coach just called and said he checked everything out with the league director, and if you want to play, you can."

"Oh, man! I want to play. What do I do about a uniform? Does it cost any money? When do I have to give you an answer?" Alejandro asked, dispensing a river of questions as they flowed into his head.

"No problem, Alejandro," TJ said. "Give me your father's phone number and yours. I will give them to Coach P, and he will call you tonight. You better ask your parents first, though. If they say no, I will tell Coach P so he won't need to call."

Alejandro took TJ into the den where his mom and dad were watching tv and gave them the news. TJ offered a brilliant summary of the situation to Alejandro's mom and dad as if he was a trial lawyer in a courtroom giving his closing arguments. Alejandro's parents looked at each other and said they would be willing to talk to the coach, but they needed some questions answered. TJ told them to expect a call from Coach P within a few minutes, and then he ran back home and called Coach P telling him that Alejandro wanted to play, but his parents had questions. Coach P called Alejandro's father. He told him that there would be no payment required to play, that all funds for the year had been collected. He also said he had an extra uniform and that it would probably be a fit for Alejandro based upon what TJ had told Coach P about Alejandro's size.

Coach P also wanted to let them know, however, that there was a chance Alejandro might only get to play for an inning or two in the field and get only one at-bat, but at least he would be introduced to the league and maybe help him meet some friends before school started in the fall. Alejandro's parents talked it over for a few minutes, and both thought it would be a good way for Alejandro to start meeting kids in the community. They agreed he could play and then called Coach P back and told him they were grateful for the opportunity and that Alejandro would be at practice the next day.

After all the evening's excitement had subsided, TJ laid in his bed just before falling asleep and began to worry about the possibility of Alejandro not being a very good player. *What if he is a bad player? What if he was the worst player on his team back in Texas? What if he can't hit? But, wait a minute, he played shortstop. You put your best defensive player at shortstop. And hitting, well heck, I can't hit Devlin King, either. Who can?* After reasoning with himself, TJ decided it would work out then drifted off to a peaceful night's sleep.

8

The Tigers arrived at a much-improved field on Friday afternoon. Since early that morning, the volunteers had worked tirelessly, pushing water off the field and then putting down the fast-dry dirt compound. They did a superb job of getting the entire field close to being ready for the championship on Saturday.

Coach P told the team about Wade and that he went to see him. Coach P said Wade was in good spirits. Several groans were audible from the players. Wade was solid at his position. The team could always count on his steady defense. Mikey Anderson then asked Coach P if he had heard anything about Devlin playing in the championship.

"He is pitching," Coach P said, unhappy about delivering that message. It was bad enough to be missing their starting shortstop but now having to go against the best pitcher in the state without him. More groans.

"Dang, Coach P, You, are just full of good news," said Scrap sarcastically.

Coach P shot Scrap a look as if to say, don't go there, then formally introduced Alejandro. He said he would work out Alejandro and a couple of others at shortstop to see what the best combination would be going forward for the infield. They might have to use Alejandro in the outfield and Billy in the infield. There were several options, and they would have to explore them throughout practice to see which would work the best for the team. Reno Ivey would be the starting pitcher.

Coach P wanted to have the infield to himself to look at the combinations at shortstop closely. He had the infielders go to their positions and placed Alejandro and Billy at shortstop. Coach P then had the outfielders work out separately, with his two assistants hitting flyballs. Coach P hit groundballs beginning at third base as he always did, moving around the horn. When he hit to short, Billy fielded the first grounder cleanly and made an accurate throw to first base. Coach P then hit a hard grounder to Alejandro, who had to move several feet towards third, backhand it, plant his feet, and with strong athletic form, threw a laser to first base. Coach P knew then they would be okay.

After two more grounders, he stayed with Alejandro and moved Billy back to the outfield. It was obvious that Alejandro not only was steady with the glove, but his arm from the hole was stronger than Billy's arm. But, could Alejandro hit? The Tigers had gotten lucky. It would certainly be a marvelous bonus if he could.

After infield practice, groups of three went into the cages for batting practice. Others worked on bunting at home plate. When Alejandro's turn to hit arrived, he immediately lined the first pitch he saw hard right back from where it came. He was a line-drive hitter.

Coach P walked over to TJ and, grinning, said, "Thanks, TJ." TJ had a big smile on his face as well. Not only because Alejandro was a good player but because TJ had not hurt his team by bringing in a poor player. The smile on TJ's face was one of just pure relief.

During the entire practice, Landy did what she was expected to do. She fielded grounders, made nice stretches at first base, and delivered good throws. But there were few smiles from her, if any, and no enthusiasm. She was just going through the motions. Coach P felt like she might need to talk. As the assistant coaches worked several drills with the other players finishing up practice, Coach P asked Landy to sit with him in the dugout.

“How are you, kiddo?” he asked.

"Okay," she replied, but unconvincingly.

"Landy. I can tell you are hurting. And that's okay. You were close to your grandfather, weren’t you?”

"Very close. I learned a lot about baseball from him. We would watch games together on tv, and he took my brother and me to our first professional game. I wanted him to come to the championship and see me play. And now, he won't ever see me play again," she said, choking back tears.

“I understand how you are feeling, Landy. I lost my dad a few years ago,” Coach P said. “He was only 56-years old. Cancer. Just out of nowhere, it seemed. He was always healthy, but they found he was already very sick through a regular checkup at the doctor. He was the one who taught baseball to me. He bought me my first glove when I was seven. It was an outfielder's glove. It was three times too big for me, for sure," Coach P said with a smile, trying to soothe Landy's pain. "Still remember it like it was yesterday. He taught me how to catch, throw, hit, you name it. He would come to all of my games whenever he wasn't working. When he passed away, I was twenty-one years old and playing in a semi-pro league. His funeral was on a Saturday morning. That night I had an important game. I was torn about playing. I wanted to, but I felt it wouldn't be right. I didn't want to be disrespectful to my mom or him. But then my mom told me that my dad, more than anything, loved watching me play and that he would be sad if I missed my game because of his passing. She said he would have wanted me to play because he knew how much I loved baseball. It was the one thing that we shared in a big way that we could talk about together."

Coach P then leaned towards her, wrapping his arm around her shoulders, and in a fatherly tone said, "So, here's what I am telling you, Landy. Your grandfather would be sad as well if he thought you lost your love and your enthusiasm for baseball. I never met your grandfather, but I know with one-hundred percent certainty, he would want you to give everything you have and enjoy it like you always have," Coach P said, pointing out towards first base. "Will it be tough? Sure. No doubt about it. It was tough for me, too. There weren't many moments in that game I played that night when I didn't think of my dad, and you will feel the same tomorrow. I played my heart out that game. I dedicated the game to him. Landy, that is what your grandfather would have wanted. You have worked hard to get to this point to play in a championship game. I also believe he will be with you in spirit. I just know it."

Landy nodded, wiping away tears rolling down her cheeks. “Thanks, Coach,” she said as she hugged him and then joined her teammates.

9

TJ's mom let him sleep in later than usual on Saturday morning before calling him to breakfast. The aroma of pancakes and sizzling bacon from the kitchen drifted throughout the two-story, brick, three-bedroom house until it found its way into TJ's room, waking him up. His mom, without exception, always cooked his favorite breakfast of blueberry pancakes and bacon on Saturdays during baseball season. Tonight's championship game would be played later at 7 p.m. because there were no other games that day.

TJ couldn't wait for the final game of the season. Typically, he was not a big breakfast eater, except on game days. After devouring five pancakes and four strips of bacon, TJ retreated to the family room where he watched on the big screen tv many of the previous night's major league baseball highlights on ESPN. Even on school mornings, just after breakfast, TJ would spend time viewing the events of the last day's games to see how Dansby and the Braves made out.

He had developed his genuine love for baseball in the second grade. His dad had played baseball for many years up through college and took TJ to many Braves games. Although he loved the game and wanted TJ to play, he never pushed baseball on him or forced him to play. He just introduced TJ to the game with a new glove and baseball just like his father had done with him, then played catch with him in the backyard. Baseball took hold of TJ quickly. He loved all things baseball. It was in his blood.

After watching the highlights on ESPN for a bit, TJ changed out of his pajamas and pulled on a pair of faded blue jeans, a white t-shirt, laced up his tennis shoes, then put his Tigers' baseball cap on and headed for the front door.

"Mom, I'm heading to the movies now," he said.

"Okay. Have a good time, be careful, be safe and come right home afterward. You need to rest for the game tonight," his mom replied. "And don't fill up on popcorn!"

"Yes, mam," said TJ as he dashed out the front door offering Grounder a soft pat on the head as he left.

Almost every Saturday morning, many of the school kids from the middle and elementary schools could be found at the local theatre. For TJ and many of the kids, the theatre was within walking distance of their neighborhood.

This day will rock, thought TJ. *A movie in the morning, watch the Braves play an afternoon game on tv, and play the championship game that night*. And, more importantly, no more school for two months!

Summer was finally here. Nothing but pick-up baseball games, swimming at the community pool, and hanging out with his friends. Of course, there would be daily chores to take care of, but better than homework every day. He could knock those out right after breakfast.

From his house, it took TJ precisely 15 minutes to walk to the local multiplex cinema, which offered eight screens. He always met his friends outside the theatre before buying their tickets because sometimes, they wouldn't decide what movie to see until the last minute. Today, the movie had already been decided by Scrap: *King Kong*.

As TJ approached his pals, he noticed Devlin and a handful of Reds' players in their Reds' baseball caps walking up to the ticket window. Devlin did not see TJ and his friends because he was too busy yapping about something or bragging about a latest feat.

"Well, I guess Devlin's punishment is over," said Landy dejectedly.

TJ, Landy, and Scrap purchased their tickets and immediately went to the concession stand where they each bought their usual: a medium bucket of popcorn drenched in butter, a box of Milk Duds, and a large soda before heading into theatre number three.

"Hold on a second," Scrap said, as they were about to find seats. "I'll be right back."

"Where is he going now?" Landy asked TJ.

"Beats me," TJ replied.

Five minutes later, Scrap returned with a large bag of black licorice as TJ and Landy waited at the back of the theatre. Landy just shook her head in disbelief.

"You know you have a big game tonight, lunkhead?" Landy said.

“Yep! Can’t wait,” Scrap replied, not caring one bit about Landy's concern for his enormous appetite.

"Wow. The theatre is packed," declared TJ as they stood in the back, scanning over the rows of seats to find several together.

“There are three seats right there. Let’s grab them, quick,” Scrap said excitedly, pointing to one of the back rows as the lights had already dimmed.

After plopping down in their seats and getting their drinks and snacks situated, they noticed the four boys sitting directly in the row in front of them were, of course, "The King" and his royal subjects.

"Great, just great," sighed TJ, discouraged by having to sit near Devlin and his buddies. "Let’s move.”

“No way, Jose,” Scrap replied with a mischievous grin on his face as the previews of coming attractions began to roll.

"Let's have a little fun," Scrap added, pointing to the back of Devlin's head.

"No, Scrap," said TJ. "No way. You've caused enough problems the last week."

“Come on, Scrap. I want to watch the movie,” echoed Landy.

“No problem, L. I promise I won’t say a word.”

It took only several minutes into the movie before Scrap could no longer contain himself. Out of the corner of his eye, TJ caught sight of a few pieces of butter-soaked popcorn flying in front of him towards Devlin, popping him in the neck. Devlin scratched at his neck without looking back. After a minute or two, another piece of popcorn flew again in the same direction and landed in Devlin's lap. This time Devlin turned around to see who was throwing the popcorn.

"You!" said Devlin glaring at Scrap, overwhelmingly surprised to see his number one nemesis sitting right behind him in the theatre. "When this movie is over, YOU are mine!"

"What are you talking about?" Scrap whispered loudly, shrugging his shoulders and looking perplexed but knowing he was instigating a troublesome event.

"You know what I'm talking about, "Crap Head," Devlin replied. "If you, do it again, I will jump over these seats and stick your head in that bucket of popcorn."

"Scrap, you said you wouldn't say a word," Landy whispered loudly, quite irritated, reminding him of his earlier promise.

"I didn't say anything. I just threw popcorn," Scrap said, working his way around the truth.

Landy turned away from Scrap back towards the movie but shook her head. Scrap, leaning up in his seat, continued with his quest to harass Devlin, saying in a low volume, "Hey, I just realized King, this movie is about you. King......King Kong! Ape Man," said Scrap, adding ape sounds for good measure.

"Shhhhhhh!" hushed an irritated parent of some kids sitting nearby. "We can't hear the movie. I'm going to call the usher if you don't stop talking."

Scrap sat back in his seat but continued to pelt Devlin with popcorn about few minutes, sometimes hitting Devlin and sometimes missing him but escalating Devlin's frustration level. The size difference between Devlin and Scrap was obvious, plus Devlin was too strong and mean for Scrap. In reality, Devlin could pummel Scrap into oblivion in a New York minute. Still, Scrap kept pushing and pushing. Where this was leading was anyone's guess. Landy turned to Scrap and issued a final warning.

"I'm leaving if you don't stop throwing popcorn at him," she said highly annoyed.

"Okay. Okay. No more popcorn," Scrap replied but was still fidgety.

For the next half hour, Scrap settled down. He had eaten an entire bag of buttered popcorn and almost all of the candy and was beginning to feel queasy. There was only so much candy, soda, and popcorn a stomach could take. One last Milk Dud remained in the box. Unable to eat it, he was about to offer it to Landy or TJ but instead, unable to control himself, took it and made a pinpoint throw which nailed Devlin squarely on the back of the head. Devlin became furious and stood up and turned to face Scrap, ready to jump over the back of his chair. Fortunately for Scrap, a theatre usher was walking down the aisle, and hearing chatter, stopped at the end of Scrap's row, pointing a flashlight and checking out the noise.

"Scrap! You said you would not throw any more popcorn," Landy said in a loud whisper, now furious at Scrap.

"I didn't throw popcorn. It was a Milk Dud."

Again, rearranging the truth.

"Really, Scrap? You are going to try and use that excuse. I'm out of here," she said. "Me too," said TJ, both fed up with Scrap's behavior and both concerned Devlin and his mates would beat them up along with Scrap. They both got up out of their seats and started to leave.

"Okay. Okay. I really will stop this time, I promise. Really... I promise. Don't go," Scrap pleaded.

Landy held up her index finger and waved it in Scrap's face. *"This is it! One more chance,"* she said firmly. She and TJ both sat back down in their seats. The damage, however, had been done. Scrap had pushed Devlin over the line, and now Devlin was fuming and would deal with Scrap as soon as the movie was over. Scrap, receiving the message loud and clear from his buddies, finally stopped with his shenanigans.

Sometime later, TJ looked over at Scrap in a mostly dark theatre but could see Scrap did not look well. Scrap told TJ he needed to go to the bathroom. "Where's he going?" Landy asked TJ. "To the restroom. He's not feeling well," TJ replied. "Well, I guess eating the entire concession stand didn't agree with him," Landy said sarcastically.

A few minutes later, Landy began to grow concerned. "TJ," she whispered. "It's been a while since Scrap left. Should we go see if he's, okay?"

"I'll go check on him," TJ whispered back.

"There's not much of the movie left," Landy said. "Tell him to hurry up and get back in here."

TJ was gone for almost ten minutes, and Landy decided she needed to see what was up. As she arrived in the lobby, she noticed Scrap and TJ sitting on a bench by the window located just inside the front entrance to the theatre. Scrap, his face now white as a sheet, was slightly bent over, holding his stomach with a pile of paper towels in his lap.

"What are you guys doing? The movie is almost over," Landy said.

"He's been throwing up in the bathroom," replied TJ.

"Scrap, you are beyond belief," Landy said, greatly displeased with him.

"He looks bad," TJ added. "He called his mom. She should be here in a minute or two."

"You are not going to be able to play in the game tonight, are you?" Landy asked him. "The biggest game in our entire lives. I swear, Scrap. You beat everything!"

Scrap, bent over to his knees, just held his stomach with both hands, saying absolutely nothing. For as long as Landy had known Scrap, she could not remember a time when he was not talking.

"There's his mom," TJ said, pointing to the white SUV pulling up to the curb in front of the theatre.

"Well, we might as well all go now. The movie just ended," Landy said disappointedly, realizing the morning's movie experience had gone a much different way than she had hoped.

As Scrap made his way to his mom's car, Landy followed him outside and cupped her hands together, shouting out to him for all to hear, "That's some really bad karma, dude!"

Scrap wondered as he dealt with his nausea if Landy might be on to something with this karma business.

Devlin jumped up and looked at the row behind him as the movie finished and the lights came on. No one was there. He and his buddies scanned the theatre to no avail.

"You guys check the bathrooms and closets!" Devlin commanded his crew. After searching for several minutes including looking outside the theatre Devlin and his crew gave up. "No problem, guys," Devlin said confidently. "I will take care of that idiot tonight."

10

TJ spent the early part of the afternoon watching Dansby hit a homer against the Philadelphia Phillies, and the Braves win. He then caught a restful one-hour nap. His dad awakened him and sat down on the bed.

"I have worked on your glove that Grounder took," his dad said. "I did a little CPR on it. It's no use. It is still so soggy and chewed up, especially where you put your fingers. He did a number on it."

"That's okay. I am getting used to the new one. I think it'll be fine," TJ replied.

"How are you feeling?" his father asked. "Ready for the big game?"

"Yeah, I guess," TJ answered with a tinge of doubt in his voice and not making eye contact with his father.

"Okay. What's up?" his dad asked, noticing that something was bothering his son.

"Dad, you played a lot of baseball. Did you ever bat against anyone who threw as fast as Devlin King?"

TJ's dad paused, allowing him time to think about where TJ's question was coming from and if a truthful answer would help his son or work against him.

"I faced some excellent pitchers in the youth leagues I played in, and one does stand out as who threw nearly as hard as Devlin. A tall, skinny kid with glasses threw really fast when I was twelve. He was a lefty. He didn't have Devlin's control, though. He was pretty wild. Randy Livingston was his name. We never knew where his pitches were going once the ball left his hand. I don't think he did either. Devlin has more control for sure," TJ's dad said but stopped short of revealing that he had once been nailed in the ribs by one of Livingston's fastballs and how much it had hurt. He didn't want his son to be worried that the same thing might await him with King.

"Are you concerned about facing him tonight? You have batted against him before."

"I have never gotten a hit off of him before, Dad, and this is the championship game. How can I help my team win if I am an automatic out every time I come up to bat?"

"Everybody has strengths, and everybody has weaknesses TJ, even Devlin King.
You help your team by playing outstanding defense. You make the plays you should make. You field the normal groundballs and make accurate throws to first base.
Your teammates can count on you. You also make difficult plays, the ones most infielders in this league don't make. The game against the Pirates, well, you saved it with the play of the year. You don't make that catch, then the game, at the very least, is tied. Cody was tired and probably could not have pitched to one more batter. And don't forget, they had an outstanding hitter coming up with the winning run on second.
You have always been a steady infielder because you work so hard at it."

TJ said nothing but was taking in the words his father was delivering, nonetheless. His dad could see there was still some doubt behind his son's face.

"You know, there aren't many players in the entire league that can hit King," his dad added. "Don't put so much pressure on yourself. Go have fun. Enjoy playing in a championship. A lot of players never get that chance. By the way, I'm celebrating by eating three cheeseburgers at the field tonight in your honor," he said, trying to change the subject. "Now let's get ready and get over there.'"

As TJ's dad was leaving the room, he stuck his head back in the doorway, remembering there was something important he wanted to tell TJ.

"Hey... One more thing."

"Yeah, Dad?"

"Ah, let's not tell Mom about the three cheeseburgers, okay?" he said, with a wink and a nod.

11

Devlin King was undefeated as a pitcher, 12-0 for the season. The Reds finished the regular season at 16-0. No Ashford Park Pony League team had ever gone undefeated through the regular season and playoffs, at least as far back as anyone around here could recall. The other pitchers for the Reds were average, but the strong hitting by the Reds made up the difference. Devlin also led the league with 18 home runs. Most of them massive shots. When he went yard, there was no doubt about it. Hitting the long ball was as easy as pitching to him.

In the twelve games Devlin pitched, he only gave up a total of three runs. Not that he needed it, but he had a vicious curveball that broke down and hard away. Combined with a screaming fastball, he was almost impossible to hit. Most everyone with any baseball knowledge in the community assumed Devlin would someday play in the majors. He had size, strength, tremendous athletic ability, and an abundance of confidence to make it to the BIGS. Devlin, however, had one significant weakness. He was so accustomed to being great most of the time; if an obstacle did appear, he became a little frazzled. These moments on the ballfield were not many, but they occasionally presented themselves, and things could become interesting.

On this late spring night, the league championship was at stake. Not one person in the league, players, coaches, parents or anyone else for that matter expected the Tigers to win, but almost everyone wanted the Reds to at least have a challenge on their hands and maybe even have a little scare put into them. The Reds were always dominating, and when Devlin pitched, he was lights out. This challenge was not just an uphill battle but a huge mountain to climb. As good as it might be for them to be taken down a notch or two, the Reds were just too strong. They were loaded. Confidence was not high on the list for the Tigers going into the championship game.

The Tigers slipped out of their sliders, put on their cleats, and hung their equipment bags in the dugout. Coach P wrapped up a brief meeting with league officials and the umpires at home plate. He walked back towards the dugout, clapping his hands enthusiastically and blowing his standard giant bubbles.

"Let's get to work. We have a game to win. All-Hands, on Deck!"

The Tigers moved slowly out of the dugout to warm up their arms but carried themselves sluggishly. It appeared they had resigned themselves to losing before the first pitch.

Landy threw in the outfield grass with Scrap while TJ loosened his arm up with his new shortstop while the rest of the team paired off. Landy was about to make a throw to Scrap when he suddenly removed his cap and waved it wildly near his head several times before putting his hat back on. She held the ball and stared at Scrap, waiting for him to cease with his typical shenanigans.

After another couple of throws, he did it again. This time while he flailed his hat around, he zigged and zagged as if he was performing a little dance.

"What are you doing now, goofball?" Landy asked, letting herself show a slight smile for the first time in days. Scrap's antics were always good for a laugh or two—at least some of the time.

Ahh, she was back. Goofball. Awesome to hear those words. Scrap thought.

"One of those giant bumblebees got after me," Scrap replied. "I'm pretty sure I knocked him into the next county, though."

They continued throwing for a few minutes and then walked towards the dugout to prepare to take infield. No sooner than they reached the dugout when Scrap felt again that something was not quite right with his cap.

“Did somebody pick up my hat by mistake?” he asked his teammates. “I don’t think this is mine. There is something wrong with the inside of it. I know somebody else has mine.”

No one commented. Scrap was just being his usual self. He then stuck his throwing hand under the right side of his cap, just above his ear when it happened.

"YOW!! DAMN!" Scrap was stung on the tip of the finger next to his pinkie. Immense pain. Not only had Scrap missed swatting the bumblebee into the next county as he had proclaimed, but it had also been caught in his hat and had stayed in there and crawled around for at least ten minutes without Scrap ever noticing.

"Are you freaking kidding me?" shouted Scrap over and over while jumping around and shaking his finger in the air. "Before the championship game. Damn-Nation!"

No one had heard Scrap ever say a curse word. All stood around watching him with great curiosity.

"Get some ice, asap!" Coach P shouted to an assistant coach. Coach P then looked to see if the stinger was still in Scrap's finger but determined it wasn't. The assistant coach returned with a bag of ice and held it on Scrap's finger. Scrap finally felt a tiny bit of relief. His mom came down when she saw something going on with her son.

"What happened?" she asked Coach P, highly concerned as she stared at Scrap on the dugout bench.

"Bee sting," Coach P replied. "We have ice on it. It's the best thing. Is he allergic to bee stings?" Coach P asked her.

"No. He's never been before. Will he be able to play?"

"It will be a problem throwing and hitting," Coach P replied.

"Is it okay to give him some ibuprofen?" Coach P asked her.

"Yes. Sooner the better." An assistant coach then opened the portable first-aid kit, gave Scrap two ibuprofen pills, and rubbed some alcohol on the spot.

"Nothing is keeping me from playing, Coach. I can throw with my thumb and two fingers. I can still grip a bat, too. Watch," Scrap said as he jumped off of the bench and picked up a bat, after which he immediately grimaced.

Coach P said, "I don't know how you can play with a swollen finger, Scrap. You are also in a lot of pain."

“What if we play you at first base? Landy can play third,” Coach P asked him. “You won’t have to make a lot of throws from there.”

“Coach, I’ve never played first base. I want to play third. You won’t notice a difference. I promise,” Scrap pleaded, trying his best to talk Coach P into keeping him at his regular position. For all the trouble he caused, he was also a tough ‘Scrappy’ player.

“Alright, we’ll give it a go,” Coach P said, with some hesitation, giving in to his gritty player. “But if I feel that you are a weakness over there, I will change it up quickly. I’m giving you a short leash here, Scrap.”

“Understood, Coach P. Thanks.”

“Now, team...do not say a word to anyone outside of this dugout about Scrap being stung by a bee and having a swollen finger,” Coach P said where he could barely be heard. “We don’t want the Reds to take advantage of the situation. If they knew he had a bad throwing hand, they would be laying down bunt after bunt to him at third base just trying to get him to make a lot of throws." Many nodded their heads in agreement.

Coach P then took Alejandro to the side of the dugout.

"I'm starting you at shortstop Alejandro." Alejandro's face beamed. "Thanks, Coach P."

"Listen, Alejandro. Scrap will not be able to make some throws today. I need you to play more towards third base, and you get anything you can get. Slow rollers, balls in the hole, whatever, okay?"

"Okay, Coach!"

"The only balls I don't want you to go after are groundballs directly to him or pop-ups at him. If the Reds see you cutting in front of him and going after those, then they might suspect something."

"I understand, Coach P."

The Tigers were in their white uniforms with orange numbers and TIGERS in orange outlined in navy blue sewn on the front of the jersey and wearing their blue caps with the orange T on the front. With their arms warmed up, they grabbed their gloves and headed out to take infield practice.

TJ took his position at second base as he and the other infielders took ground balls. He would occasionally sneak a look over to the other side of the field and watch Devlin King warm up with his catcher just outside the fence down the left-field line. Hearing the loud pop of the Reds' catcher's leather mitt, TJ began to feel the nerves kick in. That was normal, though, for him. He always was a little nervous before a game, especially when watching the opposing pitcher warm-up, which was a habit. Sometimes the other team's pitcher would be someone that TJ hit well, and he would feel hopeful he would have a good night at the plate. TJ would feel a bit shaky when a hard-throwing pitcher would be warming up, especially when the pops were louder than most as they hit the catcher's mitt. Devlin King's pops were at the highest "pop" level. Scary loud. It didn't matter if it was a big important game or not. TJ's dad had told him, you need always be a little nervous. It gets the adrenalin flowing and prepares you to perform.

The Tigers did not look like a team playing in the league championship game as they took infield practice. They all appeared to be uptight. Coach P hit infield practice, but everyone except Alejandro fumbled grounders and frequently threw wildly to first base, including Scrap. The Reds laughed and pointed at Scrap when he tripped over the third-base bag while taking a throw from the outfield.

"Hey, Crap Head!" yelled Devlin King from the Reds' bullpen as he ended his warm-ups and headed towards the dugout. "Watch out for that white square. It's called third base!" Devlin said, ragging on his sworn enemy.

Scrap, embarrassed, did not look in Devlin’s direction.

Coach P could see the nervousness and abruptly halted infield practice. "Everybody, hustle in. Let's Go!" he shouted, calling the entire team to gather between the pitcher's mound and second base.

Leaning on his bat, he paused before speaking. After a short time of letting his players stand there and collect themselves, he began to speak commandingly.

"You won 14 out of 16 games this season," Coach P said firmly. "Did the league director award you those wins for just showing up?"

"No, Coach P," replied Diesel as he pounded a fist into his catcher's mitt.

"Absolutely not! You won every one of them yourselves by playing outstanding baseball. Get back to your positions and play like you deserve to be here. Understood?" Coach P said finishing what he hoped would be a bit of a kick in the pants speech.

Coach P's brief words seemed to work as they all pepped up as they ran back to their positions to finish infield practice with a much better performance. Scrap made the remainder of his throws but not without an occasional moan or grimace from the impact of the bee sting. The medication had not kicked in yet. The ice had helped reduce some of the swelling, but the sting hurt. It was difficult for him to get a decent grip on the ball after fielding it.

Ironically, the Tigers had not played the Reds during the regular season. The two teams were scheduled to meet the second game of the season in early March, but a cold snap came through with snow flurries and sleet, canceling the game. The rescheduled game was rained out, so the only team the Reds had not played during the season was the Tigers. Now it was the Reds' turn to warm up out on the field. They were confident, and their confidence was even more strengthened by observing the sloppy infield practice just displayed by the Tigers.

The Reds looked smooth and crisp as they took ground balls and delivered quick, accurate throws to first base. They talked to each other like pros, encouraging one another. Even their uniforms looked especially good on them tonight. White pants, white sleeveless jerseys with “REDS’ printed in bold red across the front over a red undershirt. Their bright red hats sported a large white "C" in the front.

As the Reds finished their infield practice, TJ looked up from the dugout bench and saw his mom and dad sitting on the hill behind their first-base dugout, chatting to other parents. He believed his parents would probably go home disappointed, but he was determined to give his absolute best. None of the Tigers' parents thought there was even the slightest chance to win this game, not with Devlin pitching for the Reds. Still, they were there to cheer on their kids and celebrate a remarkable season that no one had expected.

Before introducing the teams and coaches, Coach P called the team out behind the dugout for one last quick pep talk.

"I’m not going into a long speech here. You all know what to do. We have a tough battle tonight but know this. I have known many people who played baseball since they were kids, and they never were able to play in a game like this one you are playing in tonight. It's a cool thing. I hope you will remember it for a long time. Play hard out there. Remember, you must play fun-da-mental baseball tonight. It's crucial. You got here by playing solid baseball. Remember that. Most of you don't think we can beat Devlin King," he said, then held a long pause. "But we can."

Those words gained some attention from the Tigers as they perked up and waited to hear what Coach P would say next.

"He has a weakness. I know what that weakness is. I have seen it once already this year in a game I saw him pitch. Hopefully, we will be in a situation tonight to take advantage of it."

Scrap looked over at TJ and gave him a wink as if to say, *I knew this already*.

"I may or may not ask you to do some things tonight, which may seem strange," Coach P continued as he blew a giant bubble. "If I do, just do what I ask to the fullest of your ability, and we'll see what happens. Just trust me, guys. Now, All-Hands, on Deck!"

The Reds were now back in their dugout as well. The public address speaker for the game announced all of the players and coaches' names and had each line up on their respective baselines.

Devlin turned to several of his teammates as they stood on the third-base foul line and said, "I'm throwing a perfect game tonight. Nobody is getting a hit off me. I'm not walking anybody, and nobody better make an error. Not one of them gets on base tonight. Understood?" he asked his Reds' teammates.

No one said a word. During the season, his teammates had witnessed that nothing was ever Devlin's fault, even if it was. With that command from the Reds' ace pitcher, they started to feel some championship game pressure, as if just playing for the championship wasn't enough.

The players, coaches, and fans then stood at attention, facing the American flag flying in a gentle breeze on the flagpole standing beyond the center field fence. At the same time, a taped recording of the National Anthem crackled over the speaker system throughout the ballpark. Red, white, orange, and blue banners hung on the fencing, circling Sewart field. The smell of hot dogs, hamburgers and barbecue chicken cooking on a charcoal grill next to the concession stand contributed to a festive evening. A pick-up game of paper-cup baseball with a slew of kids had already begun behind the third-base stands. In a firm voice, the home plate umpire shouted, "Play Ball!"

It was game time.

12

Reno Ivey was a natural-born pitcher. He was average in size, but he had a strong arm and pinpoint control with his pitches. Most of the pitchers in the league were throwers. They would just rear back and throw and not develop any real strategy. Other pitchers might walk five or six batters in a seven-inning game. The right-handed Reno would walk maybe one or two. He also had a dazzling curveball that could startle a right-handed hitter. He couldn't throw as fast as King, who could, but his pitches were fast enough to get many batters out, especially with Reno being able to place his pitches where he wanted them.

The home plate umpire brushed the dirt off the plate with his small sweep broom and then pointed at Reno to deliver his first pitch. The Ashford Park Pony League rules stated that a coin toss would determine the home team in the championship game. The Reds did not like this rule as they felt their undefeated first-place record during the regular season should have earned them the right to be the home team which would have given them the last at-bat of the game but rules were rules. The Tigers won the coin toss and chose to be the home team.

On the first pitch of the game, the lead-off hitter for the Reds hit a hard groundball straight at TJ, who fielded it cleanly and threw on to Landy at first base for the first out. The championship game was underway with the two best teams in the league on a beautiful late spring night. *Glad I got that first one out of the way*, TJ thought. *That should help the nerves.*

The next batter hit a line drive straight at Scrap, who never moved and didn't have to make a throw. A good start against the mighty Reds. Two outs.

The number three-hitter in the lineup was the second-best hitter in the league, Tyler Milner, bested only by Devlin King in batting statistics. Tyler not only hit 14 homers but hit the longest homerun anybody had hit in the league during the season.

A chubby, slow-footed first baseman, he hit a round-tripper in the last game of the regular season, which traveled over the center field fence and the top of the scoreboard. As far as anyone knew, no one had ever seen anyone in the league hit a ball that far at Sewart Field. Devlin and Tyler were the two primary reasons the Reds were undefeated.

No other team had two big guys who could hit as they could. Unfair!

I gotta be careful here, Reno thought.

Tyler stepped into the box and said to Diesel, "I'm going yard. I don't care what you guys throw."

Diesel looked at him in disbelief and said, "You are a little cocky, aren't you?"

Tyler took two full practice swings and looked out at Reno with a sly grin as if to say, throw it over the plate and watch it disappear. Reno made a rare mistake and threw a fastball in the worst possible location, right over the middle of the plate. *CRACK!* Everyone in the park watched it sail high over the left-field fence.

Tyler trotted slowly around the bases, embracing the applause and cheers from the Reds' supporters. His teammates rushed out of the dugout and gathered near home plate, giving the slugger pats on his helmet and back. Reno had to compose himself after watching the baseball land over the fence. The Reds had their first run on the board.

Devlin, batting clean-up now stood in the box, appearing very relaxed as if he was waiting on a bus and not waiting for a fastball down the middle of the plate. Peering out from under his red batting helmet, he watched a fastball catch the outside of the plate for strike one. The bat never moved off Devlin's shoulder as he stood motionless in the box. Reno threw the next one in the same spot on the outside of the plate for strike two. Again, Devlin stood still. The bat remained on his shoulder. He did not adjust his feet or his stance in any way.

"Come on, Devlin!" his coach shouted, annoyed that his big hitter was just standing there. "Be ready in there!"

"I know what I'm doing," Devlin muttered, responding to his coach's directions. Reno figured he would throw Devlin the same pitch again, not realizing Devlin was setting Reno up. As the fastball headed for the same spot, again, this time Devlin's bat came alive. The seemingly sleeping giant awoke to bring forth a swing of such force that there was no doubt about the result when the bat and ball collided. A massive shot over the left-field fence. Devlin held onto his bat until he was almost at first base, then threw it down hard on the ground in front of the Tigers' dugout, as if he was making a statement of some sort. As he rounded third base on his slow home run trot, he threw his left shoulder into Scrap, who was standing almost directly in front of the base blocking Devlin's path.

"Crap Head!" growled Devlin King. "Lucky swing," mumbled Scrap.

"Nice one," the third-base coach for the Reds said as he high-fived the slugger on his way to home plate after circling the bases. "Nice one" was an understatement. *That ball was corked*! Thought Scrap. Watching that long dinger made Scrap's finger hurt worse because of who hit it. The Reds were up 2-0 in the first inning, and both runs came in with two outs—both bombs. Devlin was mobbed at home plate by his teammates.

TJ glanced over at Alejandro and said, "See what I mean?"

"Wow!" replied Alejandro in total awe of the blast from Devlin's bat. "We didn't have anyone in our league in Texas that could hit a ball like that."

"Man, I thought those were good pitches," a dismayed Reno said to his catcher, who was rubbing dirt on a new baseball he brought out to him on the mound.

"No problem," said Diesel with a smile, trying to remain upbeat and keeping Reno focused. "We have a lot of baseball to play. Let's get this next guy."

The number five-hitter for the Reds was Devlin's brother Dale, one year younger. He was not nearly as good as his older brother, but Dale was a solid infielder and decent hitter. Dale was a friendly kid. Everyone liked him. He caused no problems, and he always had a smile on his face. Hard to tell that he and Devlin were brothers. He would have fit in nicely with the Tigers. His first at-bat in the championship, however, was not successful. Reno struck him out on three curveballs, with the last two just swings and misses.

The Reds were already up by two before the Tigers stepped to the plate for the first time. Scrap was the lead-off hitter and the first to bat against King. The home plate umpire tossed a new baseball to Devlin so he could take his eight warm-up pitches. Coach P had thought seriously about moving Scrap down in the batting order due to his swollen finger but decided to keep him in the lead-off spot.

A right-handed batter, Scrap stepped into the batters' box. He could only grip the bat with his thumb and first two fingers, but no one on the Reds seemed to notice. The swollen finger and pinky just went along for the ride. *This is going to be a problem*, Scrap thought. And against the hardest throwing pitcher in the state.

King looked like a giant on the mound. His red cap pulled down as usual, with his squinting eyes barely visible. Devlin was calm, figuring this would be a cakewalk. While Scrap took a few practice swings, the events over the last couple of days ran through his mind causing him to now maybe regret that he had gotten under Devlin's skin. Devlin was jacked. He was finally going to get his revenge against Scrap. Scrap was somewhat worried the fireballer would throw at him but figured Devlin wouldn't be selfish in a championship game.

Scrap was now staring directly at the monster now standing on top of the hill. The Reds' ace hurler toed the rubber, stared at Scrap in the batter's box, and peered in at the signal from his catcher who called for a fastball. Devlin stood motionless, holding the baseball in his right hand tucked inside his glove, which he held in front of his face just below his eyes. It seemed like twenty minutes to Scrap, although it was only a few seconds. Devlin could tell Scrap was nervous and just kept his menacing stare going, hoping the stocky pest was worrying about getting popped.

"TIME!" yelled the home plate umpire, who had grown impatient with the pitcher. Removing his mask and stepping out from behind the plate, he looked out at the mound and asked Devlin,

"Is there a problem, son?" unaware there were issues between Devlin and Scrap.

"Nope," Devlin answered quickly.

“Alright, then. Let’s go! Let’s play baseball.”

Scrap did not know what to expect. Anything with Devlin was possible. All of the annoyances he had pushed Devlin's way the last few weeks had caught up to Scrap. He now realized Devlin's wrath could come crashing down in him big time as he now stood waiting for Devlin to deliver the first pitch. The big hurler went into his wind up and after an extraordinarily high leg kick threw a searing fastball which sailed right over Scrap's helmet, promptly sending Scrap to the dirt, landing on the seat of his pants.

"You alright, son?" asked the umpire gazing down at Scrap.

"He did that on purpose," Scrap replied angrily, getting up off the ground while brushing the dirt off the seat of his pants.

"He is probably just a little revved up because it is the championship game," the umpire said. Scrap knew differently.

"Ball one," announced the umpire while registering the count on the clicker in his hand.

The next pitch was also a blazing fastball, but this time it nailed Scrap square in the ribs on his left side. Groans could be heard from around the stands. Scrap dropped his bat and grabbed his side. Tears began to well up, but he fought hard to keep from crying. He did not want Devlin to know how badly he was hurting.

Well, there it is, thought Scrap. *Bad karma. I had it coming. A bee sting, and now I just got hit with a Devlin fastball. All within the last hour. Dang, it all! And dang Landy, too! I hate frigging KARMA!*

"You okay, son?" asked the umpire. Scrap nodded.

"Take your base!" the home plate umpire said to Scrap while pointing the way to first.

Coach P ran out immediately to check on Scrap and began to walk up the first-base line with him. Scrap, still trying his absolute best to hold back tears would not make eye contact with Coach P as he knew he would lose it if he did. Scrap wanted to rub his ribs as this one hurt but he would not give Devlin the satisfaction of knowing he had succeeded in his quest to get revenge on Scrap.

Coach P could tell Scrap was trying to maintain control, so he just patted him on the rear end and said, "Go get 'em, kiddo!"

Scrap said nothing, just biting his lower lip. He stood on first base but felt the sting of that screaming fastball getting worse. Scrap had been hit by pitches before, but this one was the first one ever from Devlin. Scrap had wondered for days what it would feel like to be hit by one of Devlin's fastballs, and now he knew. This one reeked. It made him feel like his whole left side was on fire. It didn't help either, knowing that Devlin's fastball had significant payback behind it plus, he was already hurting from the bee sting.

Could this day get any worse? Scrap questioned the baseball karma gods.

King walked off the mound, moving towards first base, rubbing down a new baseball. He stared at Scrap and said, "Take that, Crap Head!"

Scrap, in a severe amount of discomfort could not make out what Devlin said but Scrap knew he had just paid a hefty price. Scrap glared back at King and said the first thing that came to mind.

"There goes your perfect game, Mojombo," even though Scrap was utterly unaware of Devlin's prediction to his Reds teammates before the start of the game.

Devlin grabbed a handful of dirt on the mound and threw it down in disgust. He seemed to be a little agitated with the realization that Scrap was right. He had just blown a perfect game by giving up a walk. Devlin then picked up the rosin bag, rolled it around in his hand for a few seconds and then threw it down hard on the back of the mound, still irritated that Scrap had pointed out to him his dream of pitching a perfect championship game had vanished with the first batter. He stomped around, kicking dirt and trying to calm down before taking the rubber.

Now it was TJ's turn. Because TJ was smaller than most players, he presented a difficult strike zone for Devlin. Plus, TJ had an excellent eye when he was in the batter's box. He squatted more than usual in the batter's box to make it hard for Devlin to throw strikes. Even though TJ did not have much power, he batted second in the batting order in many of the Tigers' games because he could work a walk or lay a bunt down to move the runner over.

After seeing what just happened to Scrap and knowing Devlin was very aware that TJ and Scrap were good friends, TJ feared he might get walloped with a fastball, too. He checked with Coach P in the third-base coaching box for his signals. With Scrap now on first base,

TJ thought Coach P might give him the bunt signal to get Scrap into scoring position.

Instead, Coach P gave TJ the take sign. He wanted TJ to let the first pitch go by to see if Devlin could hit the strike zone with TJ in a squatting position. TJ followed his coach's directions watching the next fastball miss. Devlin was still fuming inside, over blowing his perfect game and nearly sailed the first pitch over the catcher's outstretched mitt.

"Ball one," called the umpire. TJ checked with his coach again for signs and received the take sign again. Again, he let the pitch go by without a swing. High and outside. TJ now knew Coach P's strategy for him. He wanted King to have to throw a strike before he would allow TJ to swing.

The next two pitches were both high and called balls. There were now two runners on base. Devlin had not thrown a strike to the first two batters for the Tigers. He did not start the championship game like he wanted to as he let his desire for revenge overtake his control.

"Settle down, Devlin, and just throw strikes!" his coach raised his voice to him from the Reds' dugout. Devlin did not look at his coach but instead kept his eyes focused on the new batter.

Now with two runners on base and nobody out, right-handed hitting left fielder Billy Laskey hit a hard grounder on the first pitch to the Reds' shortstop, who stepped on second base getting the force out on TJ and then threw to first base for a double-play. Scrap was able to advance to third base during the play. Two outs.

Nick Oliver was the best power-hitter for the Tigers. Batting clean-up, the strong, right-handed hitter had hit three homers during the regular season. Nick usually puts good wood on the ball, not one to strike out much. This time he smashed a hard line-drive on a second-pitch curveball from Devlin but right at the second-baseman for out number three. Devlin had escaped the first inning, giving up no runs after a shaky start.

13

Reno steadied himself on the mound and pitched well after the first inning. The score stayed surprisingly at 2-0 until the top of the fourth. Both teams were playing outstanding defense behind solid pitching. The Reds' first baseman, Tyler Milner led off for the Reds in the fourth with a line shot off the Pope's Hardware Store sign hanging on the left-field fence. By the time the Tigers' left fielder chased it down, Milner was standing at third base with a wide grin and one-out triple. Reno had his work cut out for him now. A runner at third base with King coming up to bat. Reno did not want to give the big guy anything to hit. Every pitch was important now in this close championship game.

"Time!" Coach P shouted. As he strolled to the mound to speak to his pitcher he motioned for his catcher and his infield to join them as well. Coach P got right to the point.

"We are going to set him up," he said strongly. "He does not like to walk and will swing at anything. He might try and do what he did his first time up. If he does, start him off with the same two fastballs on the outside of the plate you did last time, Reno. He will stand there, take two pitches, and nail the third one. If you get two strikes on him with the fastballs, then throw the breaking pitch."

"Got it, Coach," Reno replied.

"Scrap, play over right by the line behind the bag," directed Coach P. "If he does swing at the curve and hits it, he will pull it, and we need to protect the line so he doesn't pick up extra bases on us. Alejandro, you move over towards third base just before the third pitch, too, to protect the hole over there when Scrap moves to cover the line," Coach said, finishing his plan.

"Okay," Alejandro replied.

Just as Coach P suspected, Devlin King watched the first two fastballs catch the outside corner of the plate. Both strikes. Again, he never lifted the bat off of his shoulder. After the second pitch, his coach yelled out to his hitter,

"Come on, Devlin, swing the bat, son!"

Reno knew that the next pitch would be crushed if he threw the same one. It started like a fastball that appeared to be heading right towards Devlin's helmet, forcing him to bail out of the batter's box, then curved sharply back towards the middle of the plate, just above the waist on the big hitter. King was shocked and embarrassed. He was usually doing the intimidating, not the one being intimidated.

There was a loud silence, and then finally,

"***STRIKE THREE***!" cried the home-plate umpire, pulling his arm back with an exaggerated motion.

"Oh yeah!" Scrap shouted as he pounded his fist into his fielder's glove and then followed that with "ouch," at the pain of hitting his stung finger in the glove.

"Great pitch, Reno!" said his catcher.

"Atta baby, Reno!" shouted Coach P. The Tigers' fans cheered loudly as Devlin sheepishly walked back to his dugout, head down. He removed his helmet and was blocked from getting to his seat on the dugout bench by his head coach.

"Devlin, this is why you don't stand there and take two good pitches in a row with the bat on your shoulder," said the coach, irritated with his star player's brash ego. "A smart pitcher will set you up for that third strike, and that is exactly what Reno did to you. He outsmarted you because you were cocky."

"He didn't outsmart me!" said Devlin, gritting his teeth. "The umpire made a horrible call, that jerk!"

"That pitch came back right over the middle of the plate, son. Calm down, or I will pull you from this game," said the Reds' coach, becoming more upset at Devlin's antics.

Devlin appeared as if he was about to throw his helmet into the corner of the dugout but, at the last second, realized his coach was serious and instead held onto his helmet as he kicked at the floor. He plopped hard down on the bench, folded his arms, and sat with a look of disgust on his face for the remainder of the Reds at-bat. No one dared sit near him. Devlin's teammates could see the anger coming from their best player. At that point, Devlin's father bolted from his lawn chair behind home plate and ran over to the dugout, this time not to scream at his son for striking out but to direct his comments to the head coach.

"Did you just tell my son you were going to pull him from the game? If you do, you will answer to me when the game is over. Devlin is the best player out here, and if you pull him, you will be sorry!" he shouted.

"Go sit down, Mr. King. I'm the coach, not you. You or your son will not run this team. I do. I will not accept disrespect from a player or parent. I suggest you return to your seat immediately before I have you removed from the field. Do I make myself clear?" the irritated coach responded.

Devlin's father wanted to spew more harsh words but knew the coach was serious. He finally turned and walked back to his seat, where he told his wife how terrible the coach was being to their son.

There were still two outs to get before the Tigers were out of a jam. With Tyler Milner still standing on third base, the game was at a crucial moment. They still had to get Dale King out. There were just no real weaknesses in the Reds' lineup. Just good hitter after good hitter. Reno went right back to the same pitches he struck Dale out in the first inning and got him to hit a high pop-up near the first-base dugout where Landy was waiting on it to come down. The ball seemed as if it might catch the narrow overhang of the dugout roof, but she had her glove in the perfect position to make a basket-catch for the second out.

With Milner still at third base, Reno needed to get the next hitter, Davy Blackwood, a left-handed hitter, and the Reds' right fielder. Davy had joined the Reds halfway through the season after moving into the area, and Reno did not know much about him or how to pitch to him to get him out. He had singled in the second inning off of a fastball. Not sure what would work with him, Diesel called for curveballs low and away to see if maybe breaking pitches were Davy's weakness.

Reno delivered the first two pitches with pinpoint control exactly where he wanted to for strikes. Davy got just enough of the next pitch to punch it just out of the reach of Scrap, who watched it fall into the outfield grass behind him and a few feet in front of hard-charging Billy. The result was Tyler Milner scoring from third base. A great pitch, but give the hitter credit for battling.

It was now 3-0 Reds.

The next two hitters for the Reds both reached base. Reno walked one and the next one had an infield single, loading the bases. The Reds could blow the game wide open now. The Tigers got a break, though when the Reds' shortstop hit a sharp grounder to Landy who stepped on first base for the final out of the inning.

"Way to come back, Reno," his catcher said as they walked off the field to the dugout.

"That was too close," Reno replied, knowing he had just avoided a possible huge inning by the Reds.

The Tigers made no contact in the fourth inning. Three strike-outs. All called strikes as the Tigers stood with the bats on their shoulders watching fastball after fastball streak by them. Devlin King was now throwing major heat fueled by fury.

14

The Reds could not score in the top of the fifth. In the bottom of the inning, Devlin was a man on a mission. He threw nine strikes in a row and set down the Tigers in rapid order. King's fastballs appeared to be even faster if that was possible. He was unhittable at this point, especially with a three-run lead.

In the top of the sixth inning, Reno, still hanging tough, was throwing mostly breaking pitches and was able to get the Reds to hit three ground balls, all to Alejandro for the outs. The last one, Alejandro chased down in the hole behind third, planted, and threw a rocket to first. A dead-on perfect throw hitting Landy's glove, which never moved. Scrap could have never made that throw, even with a healthy hand.

Coach P looked over at his assistant coaches after the last out and said with a Cheshire cat grin and a wink, "We got us an outstanding shortstop. Well, I guess TJ got us one."

In the bottom of the sixth, the Tigers' enthusiasm improved because the meat of their order was coming up to hit, and surprisingly, they were only down 3-0. Billy Laskey, Nick Oliver, and Landy were the 3-4-5 hitters, and all could hit with decent power. Who would have guessed that the magnificent Reds would only be up by three after batting through six innings? Reno had done a tremendous job of changing speeds on his breaking pitches and keeping the Reds' hitters off balance.

This would probably be the Tigers' last real chance to score some runs because the weaker hitters would be up at-bat in the last inning. If the Tigers could just put a couple of runs up on the scoreboard, they might have a chance to pull this game out and snag the upset of the year.

Billy stood in the batter's box, took a couple of practice swings, and then waited for Devlin's first pitch. Devlin looked into his catcher, picked up the sign for a fastball, and promptly threw one just over Billy's helmet, sending him to the dirt. Billy jumped up and looked out at the tall pitcher and dug in his spikes into the batter's box, now more determined than ever.

The catcher threw the ball back to Devlin, who caught it and laughed at Billy.

"Atta boy, Devlin!" shouted Devlin's father from behind the backstop. The home plate umpire removed his mask and briskly walked over to where Devlin's father was sitting.

"No more of that, Mr. King," he said through the backstop fencing.

"No more of what?"

"You know exactly what I mean. We don't want anybody hurt out here. As hard as your son throws, he could injure someone severely, especially if he hits him in the head or face. Understood?" the umpire asked but not expecting much of an answer.

Trying to reason with Devlin's dad wasn't working, and now the home plate umpire was at his limit with him. Mr. King just shrugged his shoulders and looked away. The pitch that almost nailed Billy in the helmet did not sit well with Billy, his coaches, or his Tigers' teammates. King delivered another fastball in the exact location as the previous pitch, again, just missing the top of Billy's helmet by a couple of inches at the most.

And once again, Billy hit the ground, dropping his bat to get out of the way of the pitch. The Tigers' fans were angrily shouting at the pitcher. Coach P, who was silent after the first pitch that almost hit Billy in the head, came alive after the second close pitch.

Screaming at the umpire, "Come on, Blue! That's intentional. He's going to hurt someone!"

The home plate umpire then brushed off home plate, lifted his facemask, turned to the mound, and said to Devlin, “No more of that.”

"This is a warning to both coaches," the umpire continued, pointing at each dugout.

"The next pitch that I feel is thrown intentionally at a hitter, that pitcher will be automatically ejected from the game. Do I make myself clear?" The ump's words were obviously directed at Devlin as Reno had excellent control and had not come close to hitting a Reds' batter all day. Coach P nodded that he understood.

The Reds' head coach motioned to the umpire he understood as well and, frustrated with his ace pitcher, called time. He walked out to the mound but waved the infielders and catcher away and back to their positions. This meeting was to be between just him and Devlin.

“What’s going on, Devlin? Why are you throwing at him?”

"I wasn't throwing at him. It just got away from me."

Not believing Devlin for one second, the Reds' coach, who was about five inches shorter than his towering pitcher, looked up at him.

"I will get straight to the point, son. You are being selfish. You are focusing on yourself and not what is best for the team. If you do this again, I will bring in Benny to pitch."

"Benny will get crushed," Devlin replied with a cocky snarl.

"I would rather us lose this game that way than see your selfishness continue. Do I make myself clear?"

"Yes," Devlin replied, barely audible. "I didn't hear you," his coach said, wanting Devlin to state he clearly understood.

"Yes, SIR!" Devlin responded harshly.

Devlin just could not help himself. He had the game in hand but was still messing around with the possibility of blowing it.

Billy nervously stood up again in the batter's box. Two balls, no strikes, and two near hits to the helmet. Devlin threw his next pitch right down the middle. Billy swung hard but late, hitting a ground ball to Tyler Milner who fielded it cleanly and stepped on the first-base bag for the out.

On a 2-2 count, Nick Oliver connected solidly with a hard breaking ball that Devlin left over the middle of the plate, blasting one that everyone in the ballpark thought would be a homer. The Tigers all stood up in the dugout, watching the flight of the ball head towards deep left field. The Tigers' faithful in their seats all stood up, hoping that this one would find its way out of the park. The Reds' left fielder ran back to the fence, turned, and looked up, and at the last second jumped as high as he could, sticking his left arm up as far as he could reach. He could feel the ball land in the webbing of his glove, and he quickly squeezed his glove tightly.

For a moment, it had looked as if the Tigers' luck would change. They were so close to changing the zero on the scoreboard to a positive number only to have the would-be home run pulled back into the field of play. Two hard-hit balls had resulted in no base runners, only outs.

Now, Landy dug into the batter's box.

"Shouldn't you be at ballet class today?" Devlin asked Landy as he walked towards the plate to get a new baseball from the umpire. Not waiting for her response, Devlin turned and walked back to the mound. Steaming, Landy picked up a handful of dirt, rubbed it between the palms of her hands, and then angrily threw the dirt in the direction of the pitcher's mound. She set her feet in the batter's box and glared out at Devlin. She had something to prove, this time, to him.

She had played well defensively in the game, but like most everyone had struggled as expected offensively against the hard thrower. Thoughts of her grandfather had looped through her head every few minutes since she took the field in the first inning. She tried to remain upbeat and glad to be playing, but it was a tough day, just as Coach P said it would be.

She dug her spikes in the dirt as deep as they would go. Devlin pushed hard off the rubber and threw a hard fastball for strike one. She glared at Devlin, cocking her bat back, remembering what her grandfather had told her about hitting against super-fast pitchers. He said that when you face a pitcher that throws that hard there isn't time to see the pitch, then stride and swing. If you guess fastball, you start your stride just when the pitcher is about to release it from his hand. Look for the pitch in a particular spot. Keep your hands back as you stride and if the pitch is in the zone, let your hands come quickly through that zone.

So far in the game, she went down swinging in two at-bats, late on every pitch. But now she was beyond mad. Everything that had happened in the last week had now reached a flashpoint of anger with her. From Scrap's multiple confrontations with Devlin King to her grandfather passing away and then dealing with the arrogant hurler on the mound in the championship game had all merged to form a volcano inside her. She was at the point of eruption, and now somehow, she had to let it out.

King's laser fastball headed towards the middle of the zone just above the waist where Landy was looking for it. She was ready and timed the pitch beautifully, striding early, exploding her hands through the strike zone and making solid contact. The ball went back out as fast as it came in. A sharply hit line drive headed towards center field was also directly headed for Devlin's head on the mound. Reacting quickly, he put his glove up in self-defense in front of his face, catching the ripped blast at the last possible second, but the impact knocked him on his rear end. He sat on the mound; his face flushed.

The Tigers' fans had a quick moment of delight, but their joy turned to dismay after Devlin snagged it. Their sadness then turned to laughter, though, as they realized Devlin had been knocked flat on his butt.

"He doesn't look much like a king now, does he?" Diesel chuckled.

Devlin got up slowly, brushed the back of his pants off, and, looking red-faced with embarrassment, gingerly walked off the mound to his dugout as it was the third out. Devlin made no eye contact with anyone as he found his way to the far end of the bench.

The sixth inning showed three solid shots off of the Reds hurler. All were outs. That was the Tigers' best shot. Neither ball hit by Billy, Nick, or Landy could have been hit any harder, but each one found its way to a fielder. What were the odds? The baseball gods did not seem to be helping the Tigers. And, against the mighty Reds, they needed all the help they could get.

15

After playing for almost two hours, the Tigers and the Reds headed to the seventh and final inning. Reno was tired. No one in the entire league had come close to throwing a better game against the awesome Reds all season. He had pitched smart. He had only given up three runs through six innings when the fewest runs the Reds had scored in a game all year had been nine. That was a game that slugger Tyler Milner missed due to having strep throat.

Throwing mostly breaking balls would now be Reno's adjustment against his fatigue. A slow curve to the Reds' first hitter in the top of the seventh resulted in a ground ball finding its way between third and short for a base hit.

As the catcher was coming up to hit next, Diesel requested time out from the umpire and walked out to the mound.

"Listen. This guy can't run. Let's pitch him low, around the knees. He will hit a ground ball to either Scrap or Alejandro. You good with it?" asked the Tigers' catcher. Alejandro had played errorless defense the entire game. He had shored up the infield when it appeared to be in a possible mess just days before with the loss of Wade. He had proven himself and now had the confidence of his teammates.

"Yep," Reno responded.

"Ok, turn two!" Diesel yelled out to his infield teammates, holding up two fingers.

Reno made a low pitch on the outside corner of the plate, and the catcher hit it hard, five steps or so to the left of Alejandro, headed up the middle. His feet moved gracefully towards second base, where he fielded it cleanly, scooped it, and made a quick under-handed toss to TJ, who stepped on the bag and made a quick pivot and throw to nail the runner at first, just as directed. Two outs.

"Nice DP, guys!" Coach P shouted to his infielders.

"Good turn," Reno said to TJ and Alejandro.

TJ gave Alejandro a thumbs-up along with a big smile and received a thumbs-up and a nice grin from Alejandro in return.

The number nine hitter for the Reds hit a second-pitch breaking ball, a one-hopper to Scrap. Scrap made the stop, but his swollen finger forced a bad throw, which pulled Landy off the bag. The runner made it safely.

As Landy stepped towards Reno to throw the ball back to him, she noticed out of the corner of her eye the runner and coach were high-fiving each other and not paying attention to what was going on elsewhere. She gave Reno a wink and a nod and then quickly pushed the ball back into her glove.

She then walked back to first base to hold the runner on who had no idea she still had the ball. As Landy walked around the back of the runner standing on the bag, she cleverly opened her glove ever so slightly for the first-base umpire to see. He saw the ball in her glove and, although surprised to see it there, offered a barely noticeable nod.

The only possible problem now was that Reno could not step on the rubber without the ball according to baseball rules. He could walk around the mound, but it would be a balk if the ball were not on his person if he stepped on the rubber and pretended to pitch. Landy knew the rule, as her grandfather had told her about a similar play he had pulled when he had played in a high school game. The "old hidden-ball trick" as it came to be known throughout baseball history. Landy knew the rule...but did Reno?

She motioned to Reno with her head and eyes towards second base, trying to get Reno to move that way and stay away from the rubber. Reno appeared to be fully aware of what was going on. He walked to the back of the mound, and as he turned around and looked out towards center field, he pretended to be rubbing the baseball inside his glove, just waiting for the Reds' runner on first to get off the base and take the lead. Landy set up in her angled position to hold the runner on first. Reno started to walk slowly back up to the top of the mound. Before he reached the pitching rubber, the Reds runner jumped off first base to grab his lead. When he did, Landy pulled the ball out of her glove and tagged him on the back with a heavy force, almost knocking him over as she wanted there to be no doubt, she had tagged him.

"*OUT*!" called the first-base umpire, who had been paying very close attention after he had seen the ball in her glove.

"Hey," the Reds' first-base coach shouted angrily at the umpire. "She can't do that. There was time called."

"There was no time called," replied the ump with authority. "Of course, there was blue," said the coach waving his arms and jumping around in frustration.

"Well, then who called time? I didn't. You didn't. The pitcher didn't. Neither you or the runner were paying attention. Time was never called. The runner is out."

The umpire tried to remain neutral and not show favoritism in calling the game. Although he kept his emotions to himself, he could not help but feel a little satisfied in calling the Reds out, not only because they were such a dominating team but because of their over-confidence. After all, he was only human.

Upon seeing the situation transpire, the head coach of the Reds quickly hustled over to first base from his third-base coaching box.

"The pitcher was on the mound, blue," he shouted at the first base ump. "That's a balk!"

"He was on the mound, but he never stepped on the rubber or pretended to pitch," replied the umpire calmly, candidly enjoying every minute of the event.

"I was watching, coach. She showed me the ball in her glove while your coach and runner were not paying attention," the first base umpire reiterated.

The Reds' head coach turned to the home plate umpire in hopes of gaining his support. No dice. The home plate umpire supported the call at first base. Out!

Now, realizing it was a lost cause, the coach turned without saying a word and walked dejectedly back to the dugout. He knew the Reds had messed up badly. The Tigers' fans cheered loudly. Coach P had noticed what Landy was doing with the hidden ball but kept quiet and waited. For days, she had shown few signs of happiness. No smiles or laughter. Now, she leaped into the air and, delivering a big smile, ran to the dugout where she was mobbed by her teammates and hugged by Coach P.

Hey. Maybe, just maybe, bad karma was leaving, Scrap hoped as he observed his friend's joy.

16

There was only one more at-bat for the Tigers. One more chance to pull a miracle out of their hats. The longest of long shots. Trailing 3-0 and looking at the strong possibility of being shut out in the championship game, the Tigers' body language showed disappointment and fatigue as they readied themselves for their final at-bats. In reality, to be only three runs down to the powerhouse Reds in the last inning was almost a victory itself.

"Put the ball in play," Coach P urged his team. "Don't try to kill it. Force them to make a play. Remember, when you put the ball between the chalks, good things can happen."

But Coach P saw the looks on his players' faces. Even after Landy's play, there just did not seem to be positive energy flowing through the Tigers. Devlin was beginning his warm-up pitches for the bottom of the seventh.

"Scrap. I need to see you for a second. Step out here," Coach P called out to his gritty third baseman to meet him outside the dugout. The team could tell the two of them were having an earnest discussion of some sort. Coach P had both his hands on Scrap's shoulders, and in a rare event, Scrap was not saying a word but instead was listening intently to what Coach P was saying.

Landy asked TJ as they sat next to each other at the far end of the bench, "What do you think Coach is talking to Scrap about?"

"Not sure," TJ replied with a look of curiosity on his face.

"Scrap probably mouthed off to Devlin again out there, and Coach heard it," TJ said.

"Or it could be they want to take him out of the game," said Landy. "He seems to be struggling because of that bee sting."

The meeting broke up after a couple of minutes, and Scrap walked back into the dugout, where he tried his best to hide a mischievous grin on his face.

Coach P spoke up and said for all to hear: "Listen up. Scrap needs your attention for a minute."

All of the Tigers turned their faces towards their spunky teammate, and every player wondered what was going on. Scrap pulled a package of Big-League Chew from his back pocket, then stuck a large wad of it in his mouth, tucking it inside his right cheek. He then put his hands in his back pants pocket and propped his left foot on the bench near where Reno was sitting at the front of the dugout. He looked like one of those old-time baseball managers from the 1950s you would see in black and white movies. Scrap blew a giant bubble and let it just sit there for several seconds, just like Coach P, then popped it.

Some of the bubble gum stuck around Scrap's lips prompting laughs from several teammates. After peeling the remains off of his face, he began to speak.

"Now men, ah you too, L," he barked out like a drill sergeant in the army in command of his troops.

“I need ALL-HANDS, ON DECK, and I mean ALL hands! Not just a few of you. Not just Reno or Diesel. Let's get real here. How many times do I need to say it? Fun-da-mentals. We must play fun-da-mental baseball. It is crucial. And hey, don't forget people, you deserve to be here. Now get out there and play like it!" He blew another large bubble, popping it again, leaving more bubble gum fragments on his lips.

At first, the team thought Scrap was in a serious conversation with them but then realized he was imitating Coach P, and they broke out in laughter. Scrap had looked so composed but then unable to keep a straight face. He burst out laughing, too, mostly at himself. Now everyone realized Coach P had asked Scrap to perform an impression of him. None of them had any idea that Coach P was aware of Scrap’s imitations, especially one of him. Coach P was pulling out all of the stops to motivate his team, and this one may have worked. The mood of the dugout changed.

"How did Coach P know Scrap did an impression of him?" Landy asked TJ.

"Beats me," TJ replied. “I swear I think Coach P knows everything that goes on around here.”

Coach P's decision to have Scrap speak to the team seemed to remove a lot of the stress built up during the game. Like him or not, Scrap was something else. With a swollen throbbing finger on his throwing hand and a burning, sore rib cage, seemingly a true victim of bad karma if there ever was one, here he was trying to motivate his teammates for a last-ditch effort. The Tigers looked ready to give it their last shot.

"It's OUR time, now guys," Reno barked. Pick me up now...Get me some runs!"

Some of the Tigers echoed Reno's words.

"Yeah, let's go do some damage," said Billy.

"We've waited long enough. Let's kick some butt!" Landy said with gusto.

Alejandro and Reno would lead off for the Tigers as they readied for their last at-bat, but things looked anything but promising. The Tigers had nothing to show for three hard-hit balls the last inning, and now the weakest part of their batting order was coming up. Alejandro had proven in this game that he was a solid fielding shortstop. His hitting was underdetermined. How do you judge anybody on their overall hitting when they are hitting against Devlin King? This time, it didn't matter. Instead of just throwing heat and getting the game in the books, Devlin pitched Alejandro like he was Babe Ruth, walking him on four straight pitches, no fastballs, all curveballs.

"Devlin. What in the world are you doing, son?" shouted the Reds Coach from the dugout. "You have a 3-0 lead. Why are you throwing breaking pitches?"

Devlin just turned his back on his coach and stomped back on the mound.

King then threw two fastballs to Reno, both for strikes.

"Protect the plate, Reno!" Coach P yelled to his pitcher. “Anything close, just make contact."

Reno was a good hitter. Not as good as he was a pitcher, but he could hit line drives and singles all day long against pretty good pitching. He usually would hit fifth in the lineup, just before Landy, but Coach P wanted him to have more rest since his pitching was the essential part of this game. Reno, knowing another fastball was coming timed it perfectly and laced it into center field.

On that shot, the Tigers' fans stood up and cheered at what was happening. Alejandro was now at second base and Reno at first base. The tying run was now in the batter's box with nobody out. The Tigers were fortunate only to be three runs down. They were now in striking distance as Tigers' pinch hitter Caz Pyle stepped in the box. Caz was a solid right-handed singles hitter who always made contact. He had not struck out the entire season. Coach P had not started him in the outfield for the last few games because Caz was still recovering from a bruised big toe. He was still not a hundred percent.

"Come on, Cazzy...put it in play for us," Coach P shouted with encouragement.

Devlin threw a fastball right down the middle for called strike one. Caz thought to himself that Devlin would probably throw the second pitch precisely in the same spot and that if he did, he would be ready. Devlin delivered the pitch, and Caz had figured right. He swung hard but missed hitting it solidly. Instead, he got underneath the ball and lifted a high pop fly to shallow right field. The ball climbed high in the night sky. It was just after 9 p.m. and the sky held a twilight look. It was difficult for the Reds' new right fielder to pick up the ball as he was not used to playing many night games at Sewart Field.

Trying his best, he still lost the ball in the lights that stood just behind the backstop. When he finally saw the ball, he was too far away and had to sprint forward at the last second to try and make the grab. Running with an all-out effort, the right fielder stretched his arm out to make the catch but stumbled and fell, coming close but could not recover in time. The ball dropped in front of him. To make matters worse, he nearly choked on his bubble gum while trying to make the catch, and then losing the wad of gum on the outfield grass.

Alejandro and Reno had taken good leads, but both had retreated towards their respective bases, believing the ball would be caught. Now, seeing the ball hit the ground, they both had to hustle for the next base. Alejandro barely got into third base as Davy immediately picked the ball up and fired across the field to the third baseman. If Dale King had had his foot on the bag, Alejandro would have been out because it was a force play, and the runner did not have to be tagged. Unfortunately, Dale's right foot came off the base just before catching the throw from his right fielder. The third-base umpire was in the proper position and called Alejandro safe. Many of the Reds' fans, players, and coaches were upset and began squawking at the umpire for missing the call. Devlin stomped around behind the mound, seething, hands on his hips, and started yelling at his brother for messing up the play.

"Are you trying to lose the game for me?" Devlin pointedly asked his brother.

"I didn't do it on purpose, Devlin," Dale replied, receiving the iciest of stares from his older brother. Dale was quite familiar with those stares.

The Tigers' faithful fans were now out of their lawn chairs, and the people in the stands were standing and cheering their team on. The Tigers players were all standing with their faces pressed against the dugout screens looking out on the field, wondering what would happen next.

"We have a chance here," TJ's dad said with excitement to TJ's mom, who smiled nervously in agreement.

The Reds' coach called his assistant coach over and said,

"Should we make a pitching change? Devlin is not listening to anything I have to say and will blow this game. His selfishness will take the team down."

"I would make the change, but it is your call," said the assistant.

"Let's see what happens with the next hitter," replied the head coach. "If he doesn't get him out, then I will make the change."

Red-headed Mikey Anderson was now batting with the bases loaded and nobody out. Mikey was not a consistent hitter but could hit with some power at times. He was more of a singles hitter, but there had been some moments during the season when he surprised his coaches and teammates against pretty good pitching. This was the kind of situation Devlin King would either ultimately succeed or completely fail. When things were going well on the field, Devlin was fine. When obstacles or problems arose, Devlin could be on shaky ground. Coach P knew that this was Devlin's biggest weakness. Was he too upset now to keep control of his emotions and pitches, or could he harness all of his energy and dominate the hitters?

"Come on, Mikey! Be ready in there, kid!" yelled Coach P from the third-base coaching box. "Give it a good rip!"

Now realizing he was allowing the Tigers to get back in the game, Devlin threw three fastballs to Mikey, who missed all three swinging. One out! Okay. Devlin was back. Dejected, Mikey walked back to the dugout on the verge of tears, feeling like letting his team down. How could he not? The first three batters before him had all reached bases. Now, he made the first out in what needed to be their rally.

"Don't worry about it, Mikey. I'll pick you up," Scrap said confidently as he walked by him on the way to the plate.

Back to the top of the lineup and Devlin's nemesis. No one on the planet seemed to get under Devlin King's skin more than Scrap. Now, with one out and bases loaded in the championship game in the last inning, the two that had battled each other in different ways during the previous eight days now were engaged in a battle on the diamond with a lot at stake.

King stood erect. He looked in for the signal from his catcher. Fastball. As Devlin was about to begin his windup, Scrap looked at the home plate umpire, held up his hand, and asked for time.

"Time!" loudly called the umpire as he removed his mask and walked out from behind the catcher. Scrap stepped out of the box as well. He removed his helmet, appearing to brush something out of it, and put it back on his head.

"I think a bee got in there," he said to the umpire and the Reds' catcher as he stepped back in the box. Neither of those had any prior knowledge of Scrap being stung by a bee. Now, Scrap was using the bee as a strategy. Devlin looked annoyed. Again, he peered in for the signal. Fastball. Again, just before Devlin's windup, Scrap asked for timeout.

"Time!" shouted the umpire, removing his mask but this time offering Scrap a curious look. He was beginning to wonder if there was anything wrong with Scrap's helmet. He eyed Scrap closely as Scrap removed his helmet, walked over to the dugout, and asked an assistant coach to clean the inside of the helmet with a towel.

“What's wrong with your helmet?” the coach asked.

"I think there's something in there, like a bee or something," replied Scrap loud enough for many to hear. *Oh no! Not another bee,* thought the coach.

"Come on, Ump......he is just stalling...there's nothing wrong with his helmet," said the Reds' head coach.

"Yeah, the faker," Devlin added.

"You don't have another bee in there, do you Scrap?" whispered the assistant coach as he then pretended to scrutinize Scrap's helmet.

"Just messin' with Sasquatch," Scrap said with a wink, referring to the giant on the hill.

"Get back out there, Scrap," said the assistant coach trying his best to keep from laughing. Coach P watched what was transpiring over at the dugout from his third-base coaching box and had a strong suspicion that Scrap was deliberately trying to get under Devlin's skin. Scrap could be a royal pain, but any team would be lucky to have him on their side.

"Let's play ball," barked the umpire, putting his mask back on all the while suspecting that Scrap was up to something.

Scrap walked back into the batter's box, picked up a handful of dirt and lightly rubbed it between his hands, trying to avoid the sore finger. He then dug in to await Devlin's next pitch. Scrap's ribs and finger still hurt badly but his anger at the pitcher fueled his desire to smash one into the outfield. Knowing anything close to appearing as a pitch thrown at Scrap would get him ejected from the game, Devlin focused on just striking him out.

He decided to throw high heat instead. Devlin, knowing Scrap had not caught up to anything around the letters the entire game, went into his high leg kick, his left foot coming back over the top of his head and threw a scorching high fastball right past Scrap who was late on his swing. King repeated the next two just like the first one with the same results. Scrap, grimacing in pain with each swing. King was tough to hit anyway, but gripping the bat with that still swollen and painful finger made it impossible. Scrap felt as though he had been in a war. Battle wounds that he would talk about for years to come, one of which was the imprint of the baseball's seams on his rib cage from Devlin's pitch. He had tried his best to disrupt Devlin's rhythm but to no avail, as Devlin was on his game now. Devlin had won the battle with Scrap.

"Sorry, TJ," Scrap said as he walked with utter disappointment past TJ on his way back to the dugout but knowing in his heart, he had tried his best to use every weapon he had to fight the most dominating pitcher in the league.

"You are our last hope, dude." TJ felt more pressure than ever after hearing Scrap's words. Scrap then turned back towards TJ. "Hey, forget what I said last week. You can do this. I know you can. Make it happen!"

Wow! No pressure, TJ thought.

Now, there were two outs. TJ was indeed the last hope. All he could do was either work a walk that would force a run home and then allow the best Tiger hitters to come up to bat, or either put the ball in play and maybe one of the fielders would make a bad throw to first base.

He had never been more nervous than he was now. It all came down to him. Regardless of what superb defense he had played all year, he would be the one who left the bases loaded in the last inning of the championship game. *Really?* he thought, *after all of the regular-season games. After the playoff and championship games, it all came down to HIS at-bat. With the bases loaded? Really?* What he had been worried about was becoming a reality.

TJ stepped into the batter's box with more nervousness than he had shown the entire game. The base-runners all took their leads. TJ looked down at Coach P in the third-base coaching box for signals but received only decoy signs. He stood in the batter's box and slowly squatted before Devlin delivered the pitch to create once again a tiny strike zone. Knowing the game was now his, Devlin, fired a first-pitch fastball to TJ. High, ball one.

Nothing but heat coming, little man. He knew TJ had never hit him before, and he wasn't going to hit Devlin now. Devlin struggled with the tight zone; the next two pitches were also high and called balls.

“Three and 0,” announced the umpire to everyone.

"Let's go, TJ!" "Let's go, TJ!" chanted his teammates, all now standing in the dugout with their faces pressed up against the screen and echoed by the Tigers' faithful in the stands. TJ did not need to look down at Coach P for signals. He was not about to swing at the next two pitches. He was going to make Devlin throw three straight strikes. It was TJ's only shot against the best pitcher in the league.

"Time!" called the Reds coach as he left the dugout and strode out to the pitcher's mound.

"Devlin. Listen to me carefully. We need to get this guy. Their best hitters are coming up after him. We have two outs and just need to get him to get this game over. He is crouching a little to make it more difficult for you to pitch to him. I want you to squat too when you are delivering your pitch. Sink to his level. No high leg-kick. Nothing but fastballs, got it? Even if you have to let him hit it, that's fine. He won't hit it far, and we should make a play on him. Just do not walk him. Understood? said the coach.

"Yeah," Devlin replied, turning away from his coach, miffed that his coach would be telling him of all people how to pitch.

On the next pitch, Devlin did what his coach requested, and squatted, throwing a fastball for a strike right on TJ's knees. His coach was right. Go figure. It worked.

"Stee-rike one!" bellowed the ump. Again, Devlin followed the same motion as before, sinking into a crouch as he delivered the pitch with a side-arm action behind it.

"Stee-rike two!"

The tension was hanging over the field now like a thick heavy fog sitting over the Golden Gate Bridge in San Francisco. Parents, players, coaches, grandparents, aunts, uncles, and friends were all now witnessing the moment of truth. It had all come down to one pitch. Would Devlin throw strike three and be the undefeated victor, or would he walk TJ and have to face the best hitters on the Tigers?

"Full count," announced the umpire, loud enough for everyone in the ballpark to hear. TJ stepped out of the batter's box, his heart about to pound out of his chest. He picked up some dirt, and while rubbing it between his two sweaty palms, he glanced down at Coach P, who had already assessed the situation. Coach P knew Devlin was in the zone now and after adjusting his point of delivery was about to throw the same pitch in the same spot for the final strike. He knew there was no way TJ would be able to catch up to Devlin's fastball. The odds, as Coach P believed, were astronomically in King's favor, to end the game with the next pitch. The championship game had come down to his at-bat. TJ's mom reached over and took hold of her husband's hand and said with great concern,

“I can't imagine how much pressure TJ is under right now. I hate it for him. All of this is on his young shoulders.”

Coach P was constantly running through signs of some sort and cheering on his batter while directing his baserunners.

"Come on, TJ, you got this!" Coach P enthusiastically shouted into his second baseman while running through a new set of signs.

This time though, TJ thought he saw a different signal. *Did Coach P just give me the bunt sign?* TJ wondered. At first, it was hard for TJ to know because the bunt signal was tucked away inside the other signs.

Nah. No way, TJ thought, would Coach P give him the bunt sign with two strikes. TJ knew that you are automatically out if you bunt it foul on the third strike. Coach P would never give him a bunt signal with two strikes and two outs, especially with the bases loaded in the last inning of a championship game. Several bad things could happen. He could miss the pitch altogether for strike three. Bunt it foul for out number three.

TJ suspected he must have read the signals wrong. He then removed his helmet and smacked the top of it twice. Coach P had always told his team that if you are unclear about a signal, take off your helmet and hit the top of it two times as if you are knocking some dirt out of it, and he will give the signal to you again. This is better than calling time and walking over to ask the coach about the sign, which would tip off the other team a special play may be on.

As he placed his helmet back on, he saw Coach P give him the bunt sign again. Coach P touched his belt first, which was the indicator. What came after the belt would be the actual signal. Coach P had then touched the bill of his cap. That was the bunt. "B" for the bill and bunt to make it easy for everyone to remember. After the indicator and the signal were decoy signs. The play would be a go if, at the end of the signs, Coach P touched his ear, either one. That would seal it. That is precisely what Coach P had done each time he gave the signs to TJ.

TJ had seen that signal all year and had responded successfully with very few exceptions. Then, it hit him like a thunderbolt. TJ remembered what Coach P had told the team before the game. "*I might ask you to do something that doesn't seem logical, that goes against what most would do.*"

Coach knows I am a good bunter, TJ reasoned. *But what if I try to bunt and bunt foul, or what if I miss it? I will be the laughingstock of the league.* Well, this much TJ knew, he had to follow Coach P's commands.

His mind was made up.

Devlin believed now he had TJ in the palm of his hand and that the game was his, no question. *One more like the last two pitches, and I win the championship,* thought the ace pitcher. Certainly not *we* win the championship. Devlin King never believed it was the team that won, only him. He was the star here.

There was no noise anymore coming from the stands and around the field. A quietness fell over the crowd. Everyone knew this was it. Even the kids who had been playing paper cup baseball behind the bleachers had stopped and were now lined up along the base-line fences watching with great interest. Everyone knew that Devlin had this little guy totally in his sights. This was David vs Goliath. The ultimate mismatch.

Devlin focused his eyes on the catcher's mitt. He went into his full windup, pushed off the rubber, and lowered his body into a crouch so he could throw the fastest pitch he had delivered the entire game. The pitch was headed for the exact spot the previous two had been located: on the knees. This is it, Devlin thought. The championship is all mine, now.

As Devlin released the pitch, TJ pivoted his back right foot pointing towards the mound, squatted, and slid his right hand halfway up on the bat, preparing to bunt, leveling his bat and lowering it to where the previous two fastballs came exploding in. TJ was perfect on where he positioned his bat, aiming the bat towards third base. The low fastball caught the bat near the very end of the barrel, which resulted in a slow-rolling bunt about ten feet from home plate and stayed just inside the third-base line. TJ could not have walked out and laid the ball down in a more perfect spot.

Everyone in the ballpark, players, fans, coaches, looked on in shock.

"*Who bunts with the bases loaded and two outs*?" shouted a Tiger supporter.

"Oh No! What are we doing bunting?" yelled out a dad with his arms up in the air.

Nobody, though, was more surprised and in shock than Devlin. By the time he realized there was a bunt, the other runners were all racing towards their next bases. He hurriedly scrambled off of the pitcher's mound towards the third-base line. He picked the ball up off the ground with his glove even though now the ball had stopped rolling. As he was bringing his glove with the ball inside of it up to make the throw to his catcher, the ball popped back out onto the ground as he never had control of it in his glove. Since it had already stopped rolling, he should have picked it up with his throwing hand, which he did on his second attempt. Devlin looked up and now saw Alejandro step on home plate scoring a run.

With the force-out at home no longer an option, Devlin had to turn quickly and look at third base as it was the next closest base to get the out. Reno had not entirely made it to third base, but the third baseman, Dale, had charged in for the bunt as well, and now no one was covering third. The Reds' shortstop, confused, had initially charged towards the bunt, but then realizing he needed to cover third was late getting there.

Frantic, as his first two choices of bases to throw to were not an option, Devlin now turned hurriedly to first base. TJ was a still a step from first but feeling in a great rush, Devlin, in a major panic, hurried his throw and threw it wide to the second-base side of the first baseman. The ball headed into the right-field corner finding its way all to the end of the outfield fence.

Reno scored from second base, and Caz scored from first. The game was now miraculously tied. TJ stepped on first base and heard the first-base coach shout at him to keep running. TJ picked up Coach P as he hit second base, waving him on to third. TJ was running as hard as he had ever run in his young life. The fans and teammates were cheering so loudly that all he could do was watch Coach P. Out of the corner of his eye, TJ could see the fans jumping up and down in the bleachers, but everything at the moment was blurry and noisy. His feet were hitting the ground so hard he was becoming light-headed. He could not hear Coach P's voice because of the loud cheering; he could only see him making large windmill circular motions with his arms, waving TJ around third base.

What in the world was happening behind him that he had made it to third base from a bunt and was heading for home? TJ thought.

TJ pushed himself hard toward the finish line.

The right fielder had picked up the ball in the farthest corner of the right-field fence and, in his rush, overthrew his cutoff man, the Reds' second baseman who had run halfway into right field to take the right-fielder's throw so he could relay it to the catcher at home plate. Fortunately for the Reds, when the throw from right field traveled over the second baseman's head, the first baseman backed him up and caught the throw. He turned and fired hard towards home plate. The Reds' catcher was waiting at home, positioning himself just in front of the plate, mask off and ready to receive the relay throw and make the tag on TJ, who was beginning his slide.

The relay throw appeared to be on target. TJ, huffing and puffing and seeing everyone jumping up and down in the stands, realized what was about to happen gave one last bolt. He slid at the same time he saw the catcher jump up to catch the high throw. By the time the catcher swiped TJ's leg with his catcher's mitt, TJ's left foot had already made it halfway across the back of the plate.

“SAAAAAAFE!!!!!" called the home plate umpire stretching his arms out.

The crowd went crazy. TJ's teammates poured out of the dugout, mobbing him at home plate as they piled on each other. His mom, dad, and sister were hugging the other parents, and kids were jumping up and down, raising their arms in the air with jubilation. The unimaginable had happened. The Tigers, a good team but not a team on the same level as The Reds, had just pulled the biggest upset in the history of Ashford Park Pony League. The most dominating and intimidating pitcher in the league had just been beaten by a team no one, even the Tigers players, parents, and fans, had given the slightest chance to win or even be in the game. Total joy flooded over the field, except for Reds players and their fans.

Devlin looked deflated. His once tall, athletic body was now slouched. He sat near the mound and looked for answers from his coach in the dugout. He was confused. He had never lost throughout all the many games he had played since he was eight.

How did this happen? How could we possibly lose the game?

The Tigers had fought back. One strike away from being shut out. Now, they had won the championship against everything stacked against them.

As the Tigers players picked themselves up off the ground after their on-the-field celebration, they hugged their families and then lined up to shake the hands of their opponents. The Reds still seemed to be in a state of shock as they greeted their victors with very soft-spoken "good game" remarks as they passed each other.

Devlin was the last player in line, and the entire time he kept his head down, not making eye contact with anyone on the Tigers. He did not even notice Scrap as they passed each other. Scrap was about to say something to Devlin but seeing how dejected the big pitcher was, just walked by him, holding his tongue, even after Devlin had hurt him badly with that first-inning screaming fastball. *Good karma*!

17

The teams and their coaches lined up on their respective baselines, where league officials then presented each of the Tigers' players and their coaches with championship trophies and congratulated the Reds on their outstanding season with smaller runner-up trophies.

The Tigers' parents went back to pack up their lawn chairs and coolers, still chatting about the events of the last inning while the players walked down the first-base line to the far reaches of the outfield to meet with their coach for the last time. As the Tigers took a knee, they had calmed down quite a bit and were now emotionally and physically exhausted. Dirtied, sweaty, and injured but filled with utter joy.

"I don't know what to say," an emotional Coach P said, soaked with Gatorade that had been poured over him by his assistant coaches. "You have made my first-time experience coaching a great one. I am amazed at how you, as a team, stuck together through some difficult days. I am amazed at how you sucked it up when it got rough out there. I have been a part of some great games as a player and a coach, but I have never .... ever... seen or been a part of anything like what you just did here. It shows that good things can happen if you keep battling, don't lose hope, and always keep the faith.

Every single one of you did something to help this team get to the championship game, and every single one of you did something to help us win it.

Reno, you pitched a fantastic game against a great hitting team. I know you gave everything you had out there. You pitched smart, and you kept us in the game. By the way, no pitcher this season has held the Reds to only three runs, not even close. How about a HUGE round of applause for Reno?"

The team clapped and chanted, "Reno! Reno! Reno!"

"And Scrap...you never cease to surprise me," Coach P said, chuckling. "I don't even know where to start with you. You get stung by a bee before the game and have to play with a swollen, painful finger, and then you get drilled in the ribs the first inning with a Devlin fastball. On top of that yet, you still played 'Scrappy' baseball. I love it! You, my friend, are an enigma!!"

"Thanks, Coach P," Scrap said with a big grin.

"What's an enigma?" Scrap leaned over and whispered to Landy. "Is it something bad like karma?"

"No, you moron. It means you are special."

"Special. Pretty awesome, huh?" Scrap replied with an ear to ear, grin on his face. He thought about it for a few seconds and then, losing his grin, shifted his eyes back to Landy and said, "Wait a minute, that could be good special or bad special, just like good karma and bad karma. Which is it?"

"Scrap, I swear," Landy said. "You exhaust me."

Then with a smile, she turned his cap backward and patted the top of his head. Coach P continued his team's praise.

"Landy. You had a very emotional week, kiddo. You played your heart out. I know. We all know how hard it was for you. With everything you went through this week, you still had your head in the game and turned in a brilliant play over there with the hidden ball trick. I am curious as to what made you decide to do it?"

“I just saw the Reds player and the coach celebrating that he made it to first base. It pissed me off! Oh. Sorry, Coach P,” she said, apologizing for her language.

“No worries,” Coach P replied with a smile.

"But they just kept celebrating and weren't paying attention,” she continued. “I remember my grandfather telling me he pulled the hidden ball trick once for the same reason. The player had hit a triple, and the runner and the coach at third base were patting each other on the back, thinking they were all that. I just had to try it."

Coach P pointed upward to the sky with his index finger and gave a little wink to Landy as if to say, *your grandfather was with you on that one.*

"Well, that was awesome. We never even talked about a play like that with you guys before. No telling what would have happened if we had to face the next hitter, either. You bailed us out, Landy."

A round of cheers went up for the Tigers’ first baseman.

"Alejandro. You were a real blessing to this team. When we lost Wade, it was going to be a struggle to fill his shoes at shortstop. It had to be very tough to move into a new town where you don't know anybody and start playing with a team that had been together the entire season, yet you fit in beautifully. Our season was over except for the championship game. And, you had to face the best pitcher in the entire state. It says a lot about the passion you have for baseball. You had a lot of fielding chances tonight, and you made them all. Just spectacular defense, my friend."

"Alejandro! Alejandro!" chanted the Tigers.

"And, Mr. TJ. The catch you made in the semi-final playoff game was tremendous and put us in the championship. The bunt you laid down completely caught their pitcher off guard as well as the rest of their team. The part that I am proud of is that you did not doubt yourself or me when I gave you the bunt signal with two outs and that you paid attention to your coach and did what you needed to do to help your team. No one expected you to bunt with two strikes and two outs in the last at-bat. You did what you were asked to do and what you were supposed to do. I know that was a tremendous amount of pressure I put on you, but you came through big-time."

"You Da Man TJ! Da Man! Da Man!" shouted his teammates with full approval.

"Thanks, Coach," replied TJ with a big smile on his face. "But I wasn't sure at first if you wanted me to bunt. Then I remembered what you said before the game about you might want us to do something that might not be normal baseball. I'm glad it worked."

"Me, too, TJ," replied Coach P, wiping his hand across his forehead with a sigh of relief.

"Team, the coaches, and I discussed who to give the MVP trophy to for the championship game. It was unanimous," said Coach P.

Scrap winked at Landy and stood up to accept the MVP award. Coach P announced the winner.

"The entire team is MVP!" Scrap pretended to stretch and sat back down, looking a little embarrassed.

"We will be getting all of you your own MVP trophy."

Everyone clapped and cheered.

"Scrap, you stood up a second ago, was there something you wanted to say?" asked Coach P.

Scrap had to come up with something quickly, not wanting Coach P and the team to know he had stood up to accept the MVP award he had thought was his and his alone.

"Coach P, I was just going to say that I think you might be forgetting the real play of the game."

Coach P had a quizzical look on his tired face. Taking off his hat, Coach P scratched the top of his head and looked at Scrap hard, and asked,

"What am I missing, Scrap?"

"Coach? Have you ever heard of the Gettysburg Address?"

"Of course. Abraham Lincoln's famous speech at Gettysburg, Pennsylvania, during the civil war. But what does that have to do with......OH, I see," Coach P said, shaking his head and laughing, now understanding where Scrap was heading with his question.

"Well, Scrap, I don't know what I was thinking," Coach P said, smiling. “I apologize. Would you like to explain to the team what you are referring to?”

"Sure will, Coach," replied Scrap rising to his feet. "A lot of you are thinking, 'well, Scrap messed with Devlin's mind the last few days and got him off his rhythm.' No, that isn't it."

Scrap looked around at his teammates and waited for someone to offer a guess. No one spoke up, but all looked a little confused.

“And, some of you are probably thinking that I got under his skin on the field today by getting in the way of his pitches. Nope, that isn’t it, either.”

“Well, Scrap, tell us. What was the best play?” Coach P asked as if he didn’t know what Scrap was about to say.

“It was my speech just before we hit in the last inning, Coach. It was my ‘Gettysburg’ speech that rallied the troops! Not taking anything away from you, Coach P. You were fantastic as always. But we needed a good kick in the pants, and that is what I gave them!"

Many groans were heard from the Tigers.

"My apologies... Scrap, you came through for us. You saved the day," said Coach P.

"Oh, and just a point to make here," Coach P continued. "Lincoln's Gettysburg speech was not given to motivate the troops."

"It wasn't?" Scrap answered somewhat befuddled.

"No. Lincoln gave the speech to honor all of those soldiers killed at Gettysburg. It was a very sad occasion. What you did was sort of like General Patton giving the troops a motivational speech in World War II. You did a superb job of that, my friend!"

"Yep. That's who I meant, General Patterson," replied Scrap.

"Patton, not Patterson," said Coach P.

"That's who I said it was, didn't I?"

"Sit down, moron," Landy said, pulling on Scrap's jersey.

"It's like I have said from the beginning of the season, Coach P, it just comes down to fun-da-mentals," said Scrap as more groans were heard.

Landy and TJ looked at each other and just shook their heads.

"Umm, Scrap. You sat in bubble-gum," said Diesel, pointing at the back of Scrap's pants.

"Yeah, it's all over the seat of your pants," Reno said, laughing, staring at Scrap's rear end.

"What!" gasped Scrap, totally red-faced, twisting his head around to try and look at his behind. "How in the world did I, I......?"

Scrap had no way of knowing that the right fielder for the Reds had lost his bubble-gum attempting to make a difficult catch. After a day of one bad event after another, Scrap had unknowingly found the one little spot to sit in the outfield where the bubble gum lay between a few tall blades of thick grass. Again, it was just freaky zany luck.

What were the odds?

"Dang, KARMA!" roared Scrap.

“Do you have a speech for this occasion?” Landy asked him, totally grinning from ear to ear. The biggest grin she had had all week.

Made in the USA
Columbia, SC
05 May 2022

59985926R00086